SI

Sister Margaret Hay holds no brief at all for the darkly handsome and gifted surgeon Julian Freyton. Yet how does she come to find herself accompanying him to Spain to nurse a private patient?

*Books you will enjoy
in our Doctor–Nurse series*

SAFARI NURSE by Jean Evans
NO CONTRACT TO LOVE by Lee Stafford
DOCTOR SARA COMES HOME by Elizabeth Houghton
DOCTOR IN PURSUIT by Lynne Collins
NURSE FOSTER by Rhona Uren
DAMSEL IN GREEN by Betty Neels
DR HARTNELL'S DISCOVERY by Elizabeth Petty
TALISMAN FOR A SURGEON by Lisa Cooper
THE PURSUIT OF DR LLOYD by Marjorie Norrell
SISTER STEWART'S DILEMMA by Meg Wisgate
NURSE ON TRIAL by Clare Lavenham
THE UNCERTAIN HEART by Sheila Douglas
NEW CALEDONIAN NURSE by Lilian Darcy
THE MAGIC OF LIVING by Betty Neels
LEGACY OF LOVE by Hazel Fisher
DECISION FOR A NURSE by Jean Evans
A CANDLE IN THE DARK by Grace Read

SISTER MARGARITA

BY
ALEX STUART

MILLS & BOON LIMITED
London · Sydney · Toronto

*First published in Great Britain 1961
by Mills & Boon Limited, 15–16 Brook's Mews,
London W1A 1DR*

This edition 1982
© *Alex Stuart 1961*

Australian copyright 1982
Philippine copyright 1982

ISBN 0 263 74080 3

All the characters in this book have no existence outside the imagination of the Author, and have no relation whatsoever to anyone bearing the same name or names. They are not even distantly inspired by any individual known or unknown to the Author, and all the incidents are pure invention.

The text of this publication or any part thereof may not be reproduced or transmitted in any form or by any means, electronic or mechanical, including photocopying, recording, storage in an information retrieval system, or otherwise, without the written permission of the publisher.

This book is sold subject to the condition that it shall not, by way of trade or otherwise, be lent, resold, hired out or otherwise circulated without the prior consent of the publisher in any form of binding or cover other than that in which it is published and without a similar condition including this condition being imposed on the subsequent purchaser.

Set in 10 on 10½ pt Linotron Times

03/1182

*Photoset by Rowland Phototypesetting Ltd
Bury St Edmunds, Suffolk
Made and printed in Great Britain by
Richard Clay (The Chaucer Press) Ltd
Bungay, Suffolk*

For Bridie Drummond, my good friend
and best of neighbours

CHAPTER ONE

'Excuse me, if you please, Sister Hay'—the probationer was a trifle breathless—'but Matron's office has just been on the phone. Matron would like to see you as soon as you're free.'

Margaret Hay stared at her over the top of her mask, her fingers feeling for the tapes which would release it. She displayed no outward surprise: St Ninian's training set a barrier of more than years between herself and the messenger, for she was Theatre Staff Nurse, acting as Sister in charge of the Orthopaedic Theatre, the probationer fresh from training school.

Nevertheless the summons did surprise her a great deal more than her calm acknowledgment suggested, since she was due to leave the hospital that day and had already taken her formal leave of Matron.

'They said,' the little pro added, recovering her breath, 'that it was urgent, Sister.'

'Thank you, Nurse,' Margaret replied, her bewilderment increasing and bringing with it a measure of apprehension.

Urgent summonses to Matron's office usually meant bad news of some kind: sudden illness or an accident, perhaps, to a member of one's family. She had planned a fortnight's holiday in Spain before starting her new career in private nursing—her tickets were collected and paid for, her passport ready, and she had intended to leave tomorrow morning. Suppressing a sigh, she went in search of Sister Theobald, her immediate superior.

They had had an extremely busy morning in her own and the general theatres, with both Sir Neville Ash and Mr Freyton operating, and she didn't like to leave before the clearing up was finished, on her last day. But there

7

was no help for it: an urgent summons from Matron's office could not be ignored.

She made her request apologetically and Sister Theobald looked up to smile at her reassuringly through the cloud of steam rising from the steriliser.

'Of course you must go, Sister Hay—I'll see to things for you. And I shouldn't worry—it's probably some formality which the office has overlooked.'

'Yes, Sister, thank you—I expect it is,' Margaret agreed, but without conviction. A mere formality, whether overlooked or not, would scarcely merit an urgent demand for her presence.

She wondered uneasily, as she changed out of her theatre gown and back into uniform, which member of her family could possibly have met with an accident. Her family consisted of her father, who was a Harley Street physician, her mother and two brothers, and she had seen them all the previous evening, had in fact telephoned her mother this morning, before coming on duty. But of course, with casualties on the roads as high as they were, one could never be certain that one's nearest and dearest were safe, from one hour to the next.

Margaret sighed again. But the habit of discipline wasn't easily broken. Her face was devoid of expression and her manner perfectly composed when, five minutes later, she presented herself at the door of the outer office.

She was shown in at once. Matron, a small, slim woman of middle age and impeccable dignity, waved her to a chair and smilingly set her mind at rest on the score of her family.

'There is nothing wrong, Sister Hay. I have sent for you in order to ask a favour of you, as it happens. Please sit down, it will take a little while to explain the situation.'

Obediently, Margaret sat down. She thought, looking at Matron across the width of her neat and highly polished desk, of the other occasions on which she had occupied this same chair.

There had been the first occasion of all when, a shy eighteen-year-old, she had come for her pre-training interview and had been too nervous to raise her eyes to the level of that small, smiling but infinitely terrifying face. There had been others, during her probation, when she had been sent for to answer for some misdemeanour and Matron hadn't smiled. Again, as the passing years had seen her rise from awkward pro to assured senior, she had come here to this quiet room in order to be congratulated on her progress, to be talked to and advised, to be encouraged and urged to further effort.

In all those years, Matron had changed very little. Her hair was, perhaps, a trifle greyer beneath the austere white-laced cap, but her smooth skin was still unlined and rosy as a girl's, her smile as ready and her movements as brisk as they had always been. The only difference between this interview and the first was that now it was Matron who was about to ask a favour of her, she who—because of what the intervening years had taught her—was at last in a position to grant one, in return for all that she had received.

Margaret offered readily, echoing the smile, 'Of course, Matron, if there is anything I can do, you know that I shall be only too pleased.'

'I think,' Matron put in, with a hint of dryness, 'that you had better hear what it is I want you to do before you make any rash promises, Sister Hay. Because it's going to mean postponing your holiday. You had planned to go to Spain, I believe?'

'Yes, Matron.' Margaret's heart sank. She had dreamed of this holiday for such a long time, made so many eager plans . . . 'I'm—that is, I *was* going to the Costa Brava.'

'I see. Your use of the past tense does you credit, Sister. But I am not asking you to postpone your visit to

Spain—only your holiday. I will tell you, as briefly as I can, exactly what has occurred to make this request necessary.' Matron reached for the pad on which she was in the habit of jotting down notes, and studied it, her brows furrowed. The telephone rang at her elbow before she could continue, and, with a brief apology, she picked up the receiver.

'Yes, this is Matron . . . oh yes, Mr Freyton, Sister is with me now, and I'm about to explain matters to her . . . I think so, yes . . . then thank you, if you would. I'll let you know at once. When she understands what is involved and the urgency, I feel sure that she will be quite agreeable . . . yes, indeed. Goodbye, Mr Freyton. I shall call you back as soon as I've spoken to Sister.' Replacing the receiver on its cradle, she turned to Margaret with a rueful shrug. 'I'm afraid I've had to take your agreement rather for granted, Sister Hay. There isn't a great deal of time, and you know Mr Freyton—he always likes to have everything cut and dried, doesn't he?'

Margaret's lips tightened involuntarily. She knew Mr Julian Freyton—her life had been ruled by his likes and dislikes during the three months she had worked in his theatre. He was moody, brilliant but utterly unpredictable, and his appointment as Senior Orthopaedic Consultant was a recent one.

He had taken the place of the much loved Sir Alexander McManus, who had been 'Uncle Sandy' to staff and patients alike and who had held the appointment for twenty years. While, admittedly, it would have been hard for anyone to step into Uncle Sandy's shoes, Mr Freyton's attempt to do so had not been, so far as his theatre staff were concerned, an unqualified success.

He was a gifted surgeon, no one could possibly deny that, but he was a difficult man to work with, for all his skill. Taciturn and sparing of praise, he was impatient and he set a relentless standard of efficiency, tolerated no smallest lapse from it. Of course, he was much younger than Sir Alexander McManus, very young indeed for such an appointment, but . . . Margaret expelled her breath in a small, pent-up sigh. In spite of his dark good looks and his string of impressive degrees, she, in common with his housemen and theatre nurses, held no brief for Mr Freyton and bitterly regretted the retirement of kind old Uncle Sandy.

One of the few reasons for which she had looked forward to the end of her own time at St Ninian's had been because it would free her of Mr Freyton's tyranny. But now—she looked up anxiously as Matron started to speak. Was it possible that she was being asked to continue to endure it?

'Mr Freyton,' Matron said, her tone calm and precise, 'received an urgent telephone call from the mother of a young patient of his when he left theatre this morning. The call came from Barcelona. The patient—a boy of eleven, I understand—is Spanish and he is suffering from ankylosing spondylitis of the von Bechterew type. Mr Freyton, it seems, saw him originally about six or eight months ago when his mother, who is American and a personal friend of Mr Freyton's, brought him to Harley Street. At the time, he tells me, he advised operative interference, but the mother would not hear of it and returned with the boy to Spain. But now his condition has greatly deteriorated and her own doctors have convinced the mother that a spinal osteotomy will be necessary. She has asked Mr Freyton to go to Barcelona at once to perform the operation and he has agreed to do so. Apparently'—Matron permitted herself a faint smile—'Mr Freyton is the only surgeon she will trust to operate on her son.'

'But'—Margaret was puzzled—'how can a British surgeon operate in Spain, Matron? Won't there be all sorts of complications?'

Matron shook her head. 'No, Sister Hay. Facilities will be made available to him in a Barcelona nursing home, Mr Freyton tells me.' She consulted her jottings-pad. 'The patient's mother is a *marquesa*—widow of the Marqués de Fontera—and she is very rich and influential. The Fonteras live in a palatial establishment some miles from the city.' She put down the pad. 'Mr Freyton,' she went on, watching Margaret with kindly, searching eyes, 'proposes to fly to Barcelona tomorrow morning. He has asked me to try and persuade you to go with him, assist him at the operation and remain to nurse the patient for the first week or so following it. He feels he must have a British nurse who will understand and carry out his instructions for the patient's care, and apparently Mr Davis told him that *you* were going to Spain tomorrow, so he hoped you might be willing to postpone your holiday in order to help him. Your fare would be paid by air and, I'm given to understand, arrangements would be made to enable you to take your holiday later and to compensate you for any loss you may incur. I don't know any more than this, since it has all been arranged in rather a hurry, but Mr Freyton said on the telephone just now that he would have a word with you himself, when he finishes his out-patients' clinic at four.'

'He didn't . . .' Margaret hesitated, a faint tinge of colour burning in her cheeks as she recalled the reprimand which, only that morning, she had received from the orthopaedic surgeon, because some small detail of her preparation of one of his cases hadn't pleased him. What had he said? She frowned, trying to recall his exact words. 'Sister, if you cannot give your full and complete attention to your work, you should not be in charge of this theatre at all. Theatre work is exacting, it requires everything one can give it, the best of which one is capable at all times.' And he had added, his tone icy as only he could make it, 'Perhaps, in the circumstances, you're wise to decide on private nursing, rather than remain here. No doubt you're better suited to it.'

Margaret's colour deepened and spread. If that was what he really thought of her, then . . .

'Well?' Matron prompted, 'Mr Freyton did not what, Sister?'

Margaret avoided her gaze. 'I only wondered,' she answered lamely, 'whether he asked for me simply *because* I was going to Spain in any case, Matron?'

'His exact words to me,' Matron returned, 'were that, by a singularly fortunate coincidence, the nurse he wanted to take with him had already arranged to go and had a valid passport. From what I could ascertain from Mr Freyton, his decision to leave tomorrow was made so as to fit in with your plans. He seemed to have little doubt that you would agree to his request, Sister. You know, of course, that normally an operation of this kind isn't a matter of extreme urgency.'

'Yes, Matron,' Margaret agreed. She had been a trifle mystified by the haste with which Mr Freyton had arranged his departure, but it had never occurred to her that this might have had anything to do with herself, and she found it hard to believe this now. Mr Freyton had made no secret of the fact that he considered her promotion to acting-Theatre Sister premature. However, she thought, with a wry little smile, she *had* worked with him for three months and perhaps the devil you knew was better than one you didn't . . . at least, they spoke the same language.

She looked up to meet Matron's questioning gaze.

'May I take it, then, Sister Hay, that you will do as Mr Freyton asks? He is anxious to know as soon as possible, so that he can confirm the air bookings which, as you may imagine, he had some difficulty in making at such very short notice. I believe he has managed to reserve two seats on a Spanish Iberia plane, but I'm not sure.'

Mr Freyton, Margaret thought resentfully, had indeed taken her agreement very much for granted: he had even booked her seat on the plane without waiting for her to give it. But of course, she couldn't refuse. He had known that, just as Matron had.

She gave her assent, her tone expressionless.

Matron thanked her and reached for the telephone.

'Don't wait, Sister,' she said. 'I will tell Mr Freyton and perhaps you would report to him at four o'clock in Out-Patients. He can give you the details which I haven't been able to supply and arrange where to pick you up tomorrow morning. You are leaving the Nurses' Home this evening, are you not?'

'Yes, Matron.' Margaret rose to take her leave.

Matron said, her hand over the mouthpiece of the telephone, 'Then may I wish you bon voyage? I hope that all will go well with your new patient and that, even if it is belated, you will enjoy your holiday. Don't forget, will you, that if private nursing fails to come to your expectations, we can always find a post for you here?'

'Thank you very much, Matron. I won't forget.'

'Thank *you*, Sister Hay. Au revoir, then, and good luck.'

In the outer office, Margaret glanced at her watch. It was ten minutes to three. She would just have time to finish clearing up her theatre, hand over to her relief and bid farewell to Sister Theobald and the rest of the staff, before going down to Mr Freyton in Out-Patients. But it would be a rush . . .

It was five past four when, breathless from her exertions, she made her way to the Orthopaedic Clinic.

Mr Freyton, punctual as always, was seeing his last patient, the staff nurse told her.

'We've had quite an afternoon,' the girl added, with feeling, 'running in ever increasing circles! And another telephone call from Barcelona, to add to our joys . . . it lasted fifteen minutes. But it seems that everything is arranged now to Mr Freyton's satisfaction. Mr Cahill is to take this clinic for him, which will be a nice change for me, I must say. He says he expects to be away for ten days or a fortnight.'

'Does he?' Margaret forced a smile, but it was a wry

one. She hadn't expected—knowing Mr Freyton—that he would stay for more than a day or so in Barcelona, once the operation was over.

The staff nurse glanced at her curiously. 'Rumour,' she said, 'has it that *you* are going to nurse the case, Sister. I suppose it isn't true?'

'It's perfectly true,' Margaret returned, 'I am. I can't very well get out of it, you see.'

It was at that moment that Mr Freyton's door opened and his dark, unsmiling face appeared in the aperture. The two nurses had been standing within a foot of the door, so that it was fairly obvious to Margaret that he must have heard her last few words. But, if he had, he gave no sign of it, simply motioned her to follow him into his consulting room and, closing the door on his departing patient, said brusquely, 'I take it that Matron has put you in the picture, Sister Hay?'

He did not sit down and did not invite Margaret to do so either. Evidently their interview was to be brief, she thought, and, having assented to his question, she waited.

He stood looking down at her, a tall man in a white coat, whose face would have been attractive had it been less forbidding. It was an intelligent face, thin and high-boned, the jaw strong and a trifle arrogant, the eyes deep-set, their glance cold. He was, Margaret realised, studying him, not so very much older than herself—eight or ten years, perhaps, twelve at most. His gravity made him look older, or possibly the tiny flecks of grey amongst the thick dark hair at his temples heightened the illusion—these and his manner. In the three months that they had worked together, meeting each other almost daily, she had seldom seen him smile and, standing there waiting for him to speak, she recalled, with a faint sense of shock, how changed his face seemed when he did smile.

Suddenly, unexpectedly, he was smiling now. He said, his tone more friendly than she had ever heard it, 'I'm grateful to you for postponing your holiday, Sister Hay. It's extremely good of you.'

'That's perfectly all right, sir,' she assured him. 'It doesn't really upset my plans. I'm a free agent for the time being, you see, so it will only mean a postponement.'

Mr Freyton's brief smile faded. He frowned. 'Yes, of course, you're finishing here today, aren't you? It's a pity, just when we were becoming accustomed to each other. Still, it's your decision and it in no way detracts from my gratitude for what you're doing to help me. I shall see to it that you don't lose financially, of course—that goes without saying. Now about tomorrow—' He went into details of times and the air booking and offered, when he called at the travel agents for his tickets, to cancel her original ones as well. Margaret had them with her and, waving aside her half-hearted protests, he took them from her with a crisp, 'Good heavens, it's the very least I can do. I'll collect your Iberia ticket with mine, so you needn't worry about that. I suggest we meet on the airport bus at eight-thirty tomorrow morning. You can get to the bus station under your own steam, can't you?'

'Certainly, sir.'

'Good.' He looked relieved. Tapping the tickets she had given him with a long forefinger, he added, 'What about the refund on these? Shall I get it in travellers' cheques for you or simply transfer the bookings, if I can, to three weeks or a month later?'

Margaret hesitated. Finally she said, 'In travellers' cheques, I think, Mr Freyton. I imagine I'll be able to make my own bookings in Barcelona when I get there and when we see how long the patient is likely to need me. It might easily be for a month, mightn't it, in a case like this?'

The surgeon nodded. 'It might, Sister. But you'll have at least one other nurse with you, I imagine—a Spanish nurse, whom you should be able to leave in charge after the first couple of weeks or so. I don't want to take an unfair advantage of you, you know, or force you to postpone that holiday of yours indefinitely. So long as I have you with me during the operation and for a couple of weeks after it, that's all I'd visualised, when I suggested your coming. However, since, as you say, you are now a free agent, you'll be able to suit yourself when the time comes, won't you? Go or stay on, as you please.'

Margaret inclined her head politely. To her surprise, Mr Freyton smiled again.

'You'll like the Marquesa de Fontera, I'm sure, and the boy, Felipe, is a nice little fellow. As Matron will have told you, the Marquesa is American. They live in a fairy-tale sort of castle, in the mountains about thirty miles from Barcelona, at the edge of a magnificent pine forest. And they live in a style to which we, in this country, are no longer accustomed, even in our dreams.' He talked on about the castle and Margaret listened, fascinated by all he told her and regretting her lost holiday less and less. When he came to the end of an almost lyrical description of the surrounding countryside, she asked thoughtlessly, 'You've been there before then, sir? I mean, you've stayed with the Marquesa on other occasions?'

Mr Freyton eyed her coldly. 'Certainly,' he returned, with brusque lack of friendliness, 'when the Marqués was alive.' He dismissed her then, his manner so aloof and forbidding that Margaret realised that, in some way and quite unintentionally, she had offended him, although why he should be so touchy on the subject of his friendship with his patient's mother she was somewhat at a loss to understand. It seemed, in the light of all that he had said, a trifle odd, but—philosophically, she dismissed the matter from her mind.

There was a great deal to do, before she could join the airport bus next morning at half-past eight—her packing to finish, her farewell party in the Nurses' Home to attend and, finally, she had to return to her parents' house for the night, where inevitably she would have to go into long explanations of her change of plans for her mother's benefit.

And, when it came to the point, it was going to be a wrench leaving St Ninian's. With a little lump in her throat, Margaret ran up the familiar flight of stone steps which led to the Nurses' Home. Adventure lay ahead of her tomorrow, but today the sorrow of parting had to be faced. As she entered the Home, her mind went back, across the years, to the first time she had seen this place through anxious, eighteen-year-old eyes. It had seemed cold and unwelcoming then, a square, grey building, peopled by strangers. Now those strangers were her friends, part of a life she was leaving behind her . . . she caught her breath as memories came flooding, unbidden, into her head.

Behind her, the vast, sprawling bulk of the hospital stood, lights gleaming from some of its windows, people coming and going behind them, others, in a slow-moving queue, waiting to go as visitors up to the wards. An ambulance drew up outside the entrance to Casualty, a man on crutches limped away from Out-Patients, behind a stream of others returning to their homes.

It was a scene she had witnessed countless times before: in the years of her training, she had been part of it, one with the hurrying, uniformed figures she could glimpse through the windows. She had worked on most of the wards, in Out-Patients, in Casualty, in the Private Wing, in Maternity, a small cog in a huge and complex machine. First in the blue striped dress of a probationer, then in the plain blue of second year, next in the silver-buckled belt of a State Registered nurse and finally, today, in a Sister's bows . . . Margaret felt tears start to her eyes.

It was ironical, she thought, moving slowly towards the staircase, that she should be leaving St Ninian's in the company of a man who had done much to influence her decision to give up her work here. If dear old Uncle Sandy had still been her chief, she would probably have stayed on, wouldn't have been able to tear herself away. But Julian Freyton had shaken her confidence in herself, made her doubt her aptitude as a theatre nurse and even forced her, for the first time in her life, to resent the discipline which the very nature of her work imposed.

He wasn't, of course, the sole cause of her leaving. There had also been David Fellowes . . .

Entering the small room which had been home to her for so many months, Margaret's gaze went, involuntarily, to the place where David's framed photograph normally stood. It was not there now: she had cleared her dressing table last night when she came off duty and had packed the photograph with the rest of her possessions. But, in spite of this, she saw it, in memory, standing in its accustomed place, smiling at her. David had always smiled at her: he had been a gay, light-hearted young man, possessing more than his fair share of charm and masculine good looks, and, from the first, he had attracted her. She had met him originally when he had come, as a student dresser, to work on Beckett Ward, where she had been acting as night senior. Over numberless cups of ward tea, drunk during the small hours, when David had no real right to be there at all, their friendship had grown and ripened into what she had believed to be love.

After he qualified and became a houseman, they had gone about together regularly, accepted by the members of their own particular set as all but engaged. Margaret herself had imagined that David would ask her to marry him, as soon as he was in a position to support a wife. They had even discussed it, when David had talked of going into general practice and she, with her own career to make, had been content to wait until he should have secured his future.

It had been a shock when, out of the blue, he had told her that he was staying on at the hospital, in order to take a surgical registrar's appointment for three years, but she hadn't questioned his decision. If he wanted to specialise, he had every right to do so, and if it put off their wedding day, at least it meant that they could continue to work together, instead of being separated, as they would have been if David had gone as assistant in a general practice.

He was reading for his Fellowship, and, aware of how much time he had to give to this, Margaret had made few claims on his leisure in the months that followed. They still saw each other, on duty, they still went out together on Saturday evenings, when their off-duty coincided, but, gradually, they drew apart.

The second shock came when, on the hospital grapevine, Margaret heard that David was going out with someone else. At first she didn't believe the rumours: the girl was a young but not very successful West End actress who, it seemed, had been a patient of his. She was very pretty, but on the few occasions when they had met, Margaret had thought her selfish and shallow and so obviously not David's type that she hadn't considered her seriously as a rival.

Consequently, when David came to her to announce, a trifle shamefacedly, that he and Pauline were getting married, the blow was a great deal harder to take than it might have been. Margaret had been disillusioned and deeply hurt, although she tried not to show it. She had even attended the wedding, three weeks later, in a London registrar's office, and remained dry-eyed throughout the short, businesslike little ceremony.

She could have forgiven David his betrayal and Pauline her deception, had they made each other happy and had their marriage been a success. She could even, because she loved him, have gone on working with David at St Ninian's, had he been prepared to put their relationship on a formal and professional basis and leave it there. At first he had been, but after he had failed his Fellowship examination, it became clear that not only was his marriage unhappy but that he bitterly regretted losing Margaret. He had sought to renew their old intimacy, and Margaret, sick with pity for him but determined not to be the cause of a broken marriage, decided that the best and only thing for her to do was to leave the hospital. It was easier for her to go than for David, and the added strain of working under Julian Freyton had provided the final spur.

All the same, Margaret thought, her hands shaking a little as she took out the dress she had planned to wear for her farewell party, much as she hated the thought of making the break with St Ninian's, she was glad that she had found the courage to do it.

When she returned from Spain, she would lead a very different life—a life in which David didn't exist. And Spain, perhaps, would prove interesting and exciting enough to ease her heartache, free her, at last, from the chains which had bound her for so long to a man she had lost the right to love.

She laid her frock on the bed and, taking her dressing gown from the back of the door, made her way along the corridor to the Sisters' bathrooms.

The party was probably going to be an ordeal, but it couldn't last for ever, and tomorrow . . . tomorrow was another day. A new day, a crossroads in her life: an end, but a beginning as well.

As the steam rose from the bath, Margaret found herself regretting that she had to make her fresh beginning in Mr Julian Freyton's company, instead of alone, as she had intended to make it. But, like tonight's party, it couldn't last for ever.

She slipped into the hot, fragrant water and, lying back with closed eyes, felt some of her tension ease. Mr Freyton didn't know about David: her ill-starred love affair had ended before Uncle Sandy's retirement, so that his successor wouldn't have heard the gossip or the rumours.

So she was still free. She would have to see David once

again, but only in order to say goodbye. Margaret resolutely swallowed the lump in her throat and reached for her towel . . .

CHAPTER TWO

THE flight to Barcelona next day was comparatively uneventful. Margaret had flown several times before, but air travel was still, for her, a sufficiently unusual method of getting from one place to another to make her enjoy the experience.

But she had been very late the night before—the farewell party had been followed by a long, cosy gossip with her mother and it had been well after two when she went to bed.

Consequently, after a time, she felt her eyelids growing heavy. Mr Freyton, in the seat beside her, had shown little inclination to talk since leaving London, and, when he buried himself in a pile of medical journals which he had brought with him, Margaret gave up the effort to ward off sleep. She dozed off peacefully, her last memory the lovely spectacle of banks of fleecy white clouds, lit to glory by the sun, and glimpsed with half-closed eyes through the cabin window.

She wakened when the stewardess set a lunch tray in front of her to find, to her intense embarrassment, that her head had slipped from its own cushion to rest on her companion's shoulder. She raised it, flushing, with a mumbled apology, conscious of Mr Freyton's eyes on her. He quickly looked away and said brusquely, in answer, 'I imagine you must be tired, Sister Hay. You made quite a night of it, didn't you? With farewell parties and the rest of it.'

Surprised that he should have known of the party in the Nurses' Home, Margaret smiled ruefully. 'It was a very nice party, Mr Freyton, but scarcely what you'd call riotous, and it broke up at about ten o'clock. The trouble was that I didn't get to bed till nearly half-past two and—'

'More farewells?' Mr Freyton put in. The question was harmless enough, but the tone in which it was delivered was barbed, the eyes he turned on her coldly disapproving. On the point of telling him the true reason for her lateness, Margaret thought better of it. She returned, her own voice flat and discouraging, 'Of course, Mr Freyton. Why not, since I'm likely to be away for some time? And since I'm leaving St Ninian's.'

She saw his mouth tighten. 'Why not indeed?' He shrugged. 'At one time you know, Sister, I rather admired you for your decision to leave the hospital. I'd been told the reason for it, you see, and I realised that it couldn't have been an easy decision for you to make. It involved considerable sacrifice, didn't it? You'd won early promotion and—'

'What,' Margaret interrupted bitterly, 'were you told about my reasons for leaving, Mr Freyton?' She was suddenly furiously angry with him. What right had he to speak to her like this about her private life? It was no business of his, but oh, what a fool she had been to imagine that he didn't know about David . . . what a stupid, gullible fool!

Julian Freyton permitted himself a brief, superior little smile. He pushed his plate away, reached for the glass on his try and said, eyeing her over its rim, 'The truth, I imagine, Sister Hay. Were you not at one time engaged to young Fellowes?'

Margaret stared at him, speechless with indignation. So he did know, she thought . . . though why he should choose to bring the matter up now she was frankly at a loss to understand.

The surgeon lowered his glass and went on coolly, 'A hospital is a very close-knit little community, isn't it? The life is something like that on board ship, on a long voyage. Everyone knows everyone else's business and everyone talks about it. One can have no secrets from one's travelling companions and if one steps out of line, even for an instant . . .'—he spread his hands in an expressive gesture—'very soon, it's common knowledge.'

'Yes, but'—Margaret found her tongue at last—'at the risk of seeming impertinent, Mr Freyton, why should it matter to you if I did happen, at one time, to have been engaged to Mr Fellowes? It was quite a long time ago and Mr Fellowes is married now. I don't see what business it is of yours, quite honestly.'

'It's none of my business,' Mr Freyton conceded. 'Except that'—his expression hardened—'I was called to the hospital last night to operate on an emergency because David Fellowes, who was the registrar on duty, wasn't there and couldn't be found. When he eventually turned up, he was in a very odd state indeed, Sister. He informed me, when I asked him where he'd been, that he had been saying goodbye to the only woman in his life. Putting two and two together, I can only conclude that *you* were the woman in—er—in question. I'd hoped it wasn't so, but on your own admission you didn't get to bed until after two—which was about the time Fellowes returned to the hospital. He wasn't at his flat because the switchboard repeatedly called him there, and he'd left no message as to where he could be contacted, if he was wanted.'

'David wasn't with *me* until two,' Margaret protested, dismayed. 'He—'

'But you saw him last night, didn't you, Sister?'

'Yes, I—I did.' With difficulty, Margaret controlled her growing resentment. This was too much. Mr Freyton had no right to jump to conclusions. Recalling her brief, bitter little farewell to David, which had taken place on the steps of the Nurses' Home as she was leaving it, she suppressed a sigh. It was true that he had seemed strained and far from his normal self, and that he had confessed to having waited for her since half-past nine— but to suggest that it was on her account that he had absented himself from the hospital was the height of injustice. It was grossly unfair. Yet David's manner had been strange and, as they walked together to her waiting taxi, he had asked her, his voice low and unhappy, not to make their parting final.

'Come back, Meg,' he had pleaded. 'Don't leave me to rot here without you, for God's sake, because I can't face it. Knowing that you were here has been the only thing that's made this place bearable for me for months, I tell you.'

Margaret's lower lip quivered. Seeing it, Julian Freyton relented a little. 'I'm not blaming you, Sister,' he began.

'Aren't you, Mr Freyton? I thought you were.'

'No.' He shook he head. 'Obviously you can't be held responsible for Fellowes' neglect of duty if you weren't with him. Even if—indirectly, let us say, shall we?—even if you were the cause of it.'

'But surely—' Margaret started to object, but was forced to break off as the stewardess came for their trays.

When the girl had gone, Julian Freyton stated accusingly, 'David Fellowes is steadily going to pieces, you know, and his work is suffering. He's a promising surgeon and he should have got his Fellowship quite easily... but he didn't. And if he makes a habit of going off without leaving a note of his whereabouts with the hospital switchboard, when he's supposed to be on call, he won't last much longer at St Ninian's, as you must realise. Not all the consultants are as tolerant as I am, Sister Hay, and if they're dragged out of bed in the small hours, because the houseman on duty can't be found, they're going to have something pretty damaging to say about Fellowes in their reports, are they not? *I* didn't say anything, this time, but, as I told Fellowes, if it happens again I'm certainly not going to cover up for him and he can't expect me to.' He frowned.

Did he imagine, Margaret asked herself wretchedly,

that in addition to being the cause of David's absence last night, she was the reason for his going to pieces? When Pauline . . . she bit her lip. David's work had been excellent, until his marriage to Pauline. But would Julian Freyton believe her, if she told him so? It seemed, in the circumstances, unlikely. She said icily, keeping herself under rigid control, 'Mr Freyton, you have no right to judge and condemn me, when you have only been at St Ninian's a few months and can't possibly know the whole story. You—'

'I know this much, Sister,' he told her harshly, 'I shouldn't have considered taking you with me on this case if I'd been in possession of the facts I've now learnt about your relationship with Fellowes.'

'You mean the facts you've invented, Mr Freyton,' Margaret countered.

'Have I invented them? I've only put two and two together.'

'And made far more than four!'

He shrugged. 'That remains to be seen, doesn't it? You're a woman, and very few women, it seems to me, possess a conscience. Fellowes talked to me last night.'

'About . . . me?' Margaret questioned, with bitterness.

He nodded brusquely. 'About you, Sister Hay. It wasn't easy to understand him and I tried to give you the benefit of the doubt, but—it seems the poor young devil is in love with you, in spite of having married someone else. It's never a good thing to become involved with a married man, especially for one in your profession, I'm sure you will agree?'

'Of course I agree, Mr Freyton. That's why I've left St Ninian's—so that I could avoid being involved. As you yourself pointed out, I've done so at considerable sacrifice.'

'But you *have* done it?'

'Yes,' Margaret confirmed, tight-lipped. 'And I assure you, I possess a conscience, and I do know how to conduct myself professionally, so you need have no qualms about me while I'm with you on this case.'

'I'm relieved to know it,' the surgeon said cynically. And then, giving her a smile in which there was little warmth, he added, 'I apologise for speaking to you of such personal matters, but I think our talk has cleared the air, hasn't it, and enabled us to understand each other?'

'Perhaps it has,' Margaret answered stiffly, 'although I shouldn't have thought that was really necessary, Mr Freyton.'

'Oh, but it was. The Spaniards, you know, have rather . . . what can I call them? old-fashioned ideas, where women are concerned. Spanish girls of good family are allowed very much less freedom than British girls of their age are accustomed to—and you're not much more than a girl yourself, are you?'

'I'm twenty-five, Mr Freyton.'

'You don't look it,' he stated flatly. 'When you were asleep just now, you looked very young, Sister Hay. And when your head—'

'I'm sorry,' Margaret put in, reddening furiously, 'I didn't mean my head to—to fall on to your shoulder. It was quite unintentional, I was asleep and—'

'And you were very tired,' Mr Freyton supplied. Suddenly his rare smile was warm and friendly. 'Tired and unhappy and rather lost. You've been through a bad time, but it's behind you now and you've done the right thing, you've made the break. It's the only thing to do, in those circumstances, Sister, and I feel sure you won't regret it. Since we're on personal topics and since you think I've judged and condemned you unfairly, I might as well tell you that I was once in much the same position as you've been with David Fellowes. The woman I loved turned me down and married someone else, which at the time hit me hard. I, too, had to break away and I didn't find it very easy. Perhaps that's why I judged you rather harshly. I thought, from what Fellowes said last night, that you were trying to hang on to him, in spite of going through the motions of running away.'

'And what has made you decide that I . . . wasn't?'

'Your obvious sincerity, Sister Hay. That and the fact that you didn't protest too much.'

Margaret found herself, against all reason, echoing his smile. The change in his manner was so unexpected, his confidence so out of character, that it took her by surprise. She said hesitantly, 'Then—perhaps we do understand each other now, Mr Freyton. Better, at least, than we did. I'll mind my p's and q's while I'm working in the Marquesa de Fontera's house and I will be careful that I don't ask for too much freedom. And, at the risk of protesting too much, I'd like to say that I've never been involved with David Fellowes since his marriage. I . . . wouldn't, I . . . don't believe in that sort of thing.'

'You're a wise girl,' Mr Freyton told her, glum again. He gave her a fleeting smile and picked up his magazine.

Looking across at him, a few minutes later, Margaret saw that he, in his turn, had fallen asleep. His head, however, remained erect and did not stray from its allotted space during the remainder of the flight.

The airliner made a smooth landing. Mr Freyton collected their hand baggage and, standing politely aside, motioned Margaret to precede him

'The Marquesa,' he announced, as they crossed the tarmac together, in the wake of their fellow passengers, 'promised to meet us, Sister Hay. I hope she's here. She's not, as a rule, a very punctual person.' He looked about him, brows drawn together in a frown. 'I can't see any sign of her at the moment, I must confess.'

The customs and immigration formalities were swiftly dealt with and they emerged from the Customs House, under the eye of a tall Civil Guard, in a sage-green uniform, who wore white cotton gloves and a black patent leather hat, and who gracefully waved them on, a faint smile curving his lips. Apart from the uniforms of the officials and the fact that the sun was shining very brightly, this airport might, Margaret thought, have been any airport, anywhere in the world. The voices they heard about them spoke in a mixture of tongues; the people, mostly tourists, seemed to be predominantly American, judging by their accents and the clothes they wore. The majority were making their way towards a line of shining, chromium-plated airport coaches, drawn up outside the main entrance to the reception hall. The porter looked enquiringly at Mr Freyton.

'You go by bus, *señor*?'

The surgeon shook his head, still looking about him. 'No, we're being met,' he answered in English, and then added something in Spanish, which Margaret—despite her spare-time efforts to learn the language—couldn't understand. The porter grinned and gestured to a large black limousine, which had just turned into the entrance gates. A uniformed chauffeur was at the wheel, a young man, with a thin black moustache marking his upper lip, his grey peaked cap pulled well down over his eyes. He brought the big car gliding silently to a halt beside them and jumped out, cap in hand, to open the door with a flourish.

From the rear of the luxurious vehicle stepped one of the most strikingly lovely women Margaret had ever seen in her life. She was slim and fair, dressed in a flowered silk frock which was cut so as to emphasise every line of her perfect figure but with such subtlety that it was, despite this, in impeccable taste, even for Spain. A wide-brimmed hat shaded but did not hide her beautiful oval face, and as she came up to them, Margaret saw that she was older than, at first sight, she had appeared— thirty perhaps, or even thirty-five.

She held out both hands to Mr Freyton and said, in a low, husky voice with a faint trace of American accent,

'Julian, how good of you to come like this, when I need you so much! I just can't begin to tell you how happy and relieved I am to see you.'

'Did you imagine for a moment that I would not come, Louise?' Julian Freyton reproached her. He lifted one of the slim white hands to his lips and kissed it. The gesture wasn't the perfunctory one of the Continental male, and stealing a covert glance at him while she waited for him to introduce her, Margaret was shocked by the expression which, for an unguarded instant, she glimpsed in his eyes. It was difficult to analyse and it was gone very swiftly, but, as he turned to include her in the Marquesa's greeting, she found the conviction growing in her that this was the woman of whom he had spoken with brief bitterness in the plane. The woman he had loved, who had married someone else and then regretted it . . . the woman who, she could only suppose, had caused him to claim that few of her sex possessed a conscience.

'This is Sister Hay,' Julian Freyton stated.

The Marquesa murmured a husky acknowledgment. She did not offer to shake hands, but her eyes, blue and unexpectedly shrewd, flickered over Margaret's face in frank appraisal. What she saw appeared to satisfy her: she smiled and waved a hand in the direction of the front seat of the car.

'Do get in, won't you, Sister Hay, and ride with Ramón? He will point out the sights to you. I, if you will forgive me, have a great deal to talk over with Mr Freyton before he sees my son.'

Margaret obediently climbed into the seat beside the chauffeur. Behind her, his face now blank and expressionless, Mr Freyton handed the Marquesa de Fontera into her own seat and took his place at her side. The porter bowed and closed the door on them and the big car moved slowly forward.

CHAPTER THREE

THE airport was situated some distance from the city of Barcelona, but the Marquesa de Fontera's powerful car swiftly covered the intervening miles. As they drove, the dark-faced chauffeur, Ramón, asked Margaret politely if this were her first visit to Spain. When she confessed that it was, he told her, smiling, 'Ah, then there is much pleasure in store for you, *señorita*.'

His English was fluent, his tone respectful, but Margaret found herself instinctively disliking his ingratiating manner and faintly insolent smile. She answered briefly, 'Yes, I'm sure there is,' and lapsed into silence, hoping thus to discourage further conversation. She wanted time to think, for she had much to think about. Mr Freyton's greeting of the Marquesa, for one thing; the implications of what he had told her during the flight for another, and . . . David. But, as they entered the outskirts of the city, Ramón gestured with a slim brown hand, casually steering round the back of a crowded tramcar with the other, and announced with conscious pride, 'Over there, *señorita*, you can see the memorial to Christopher Columbus. It is taller than your Nelson's Column in London, is it not?'

Following the direction of his pointing finger, Margaret glimpsed a tall, slender column, surmounted by a golden globe, on top of which, facing seawards, stood a vast statue of the man responsible for the discovery of America.

'Beside the column,' the chauffeur went on, 'are the old shipyards and the naval museum. And you will find there also a scale model of the *Santa Maria*, the flagship of Columbus, in which he crossed the Atlantic ocean, taking seventy days to do so. It was a remarkable feat, was it not, *señorita*, with three small ships? The *Santa María*, you know, was of less than one hundred tons.'

Impressed, in spite of herself, Margaret agreed that it was, and Ramón's smile widened. They drove on, taking a circuitous route. The chauffeur pointed again, this time to a high-walled building, with turnstiles at intervals, its walls liberally plastered with bullfight posters and explained unnecessarily, 'The *Plaza de Toros*—the bull-ring, *señorita*!'

Margaret eyed it with mingled curiosity and distaste. Seen from the outside and today completely devoid of life, it looked harmless enough, smaller and less impressive than the football stadium, concerning the wonders of which her guide waxed eloquent. He was evidently a product of the modern Spain, more enthusiastic about soccer than he was about the age-old sport of his nation, reeling off the names of his heroes eagerly, convinced that she, too, must be familiar with them. Finding that she was not, he broke off in mid-sentence and, with a shrug of his grey-uniformed shoulders, swung the big car into a narrow, shadowed alley-way from which, after several more turns, they emerged into a broad, tree-lined promenade, gay with coloured umbrellas, which shaded a mass of flower-vendors' stalls.

Margaret could not suppress a gasp of surprised delight. She had seen pictures of the famous *Rambla de las Flores* in some of the travel brochures she had studied when originally planning her holiday, but the reality far exceeded her expectations. As they drove in the wake of a tramcar down the one-way street which ran parallel to the flower market, she leaned forward to feast her eyes on the riot of lovely colour spread out before them. The air was heavy with the scent of roses, the stalls they passed all but buried beneath the fragrant burden of the wares they displayed. Beside one, the owner, a stout, soberly dressed country woman, her arms full of dark-red roses, smiled and called out something which Margaret couldn't catch as the car swept past. But a rosebud, dewy fresh, described a swift semicircle in the air and landed, with surprising accuracy, in the palm of her outstretched hand. Touched and gratified, she exclaimed, 'Oh, how charming!' and beside her Ramón said softly, 'Señorita, this is Spain, where we welcome our guests with flowers.'

He made to turn back so as to circle the *Rambla*, but an impatient tap on the glass of the partition separating the back seat from the front caused him to change direction. The partition was jerked open and the Marquesa said, her tone peremptory, 'For any sake, where are you taking us, Ramón? Drive on at once.'

Two bright spots of resentful colour rose to burn for an instant on the chauffeur's dark cheeks. Then they faded and he touched the peak of his cap obediently, answering in his own language.

'The *señorita* is not a tourist,' his employer informed him tartly. The partition clicked shut and there was silence. Margaret didn't look round. She could imagine Julian Freyton's expression, could sense his unspoken disapproval. Probably he thought she had told the chauffeur to drive back; he might even believe that she had expressed a wish to stop and buy some of the flowers, encouraged to do so by the flower-seller's gesture. She raised the sweet-smelling rosebud, inhaling its scent and then, almost defiantly, tucked it into the lapel of her coat.

Ramón said sulkily, 'We are coming to the cathedral, *señorita*, but I cannot stop to allow you to inspect it now. No doubt during your stay you will have the opportunity to pay it a visit. It is of great antiquity and contains the Chapel of the Knights of the Golden Fleece.'

Margaret, rather sorry for him now, since obviously he had been trying to please her and, as a result, had incurred his employer's wrath, answered with more enthusiasm than she had previously shown, that she hoped very much to be able to find an opportunity to see it. Indeed, as the imposing front of the cathedral came into view, she found herself wishing quite sincerely that there might have been time for her to climb the steps for even a glimpse of its interior, for she had read a fascinating description of it in one of her guide-books.

The young chauffeur's smile returned and he continued, in a low voice, to point out objects and places of interest to her as they passed. Behind them, once more absorbed in their own conversation, Mr Freyton and the Marquesa sat together, paying them no attention. Once, glancing back in the direction of a building which Ramón told her was fourteenth-century, Margaret saw, out of the corner of her eye, a white-gloved hand go out to rest, for a moment, intimately on her companion's arm. It was swiftly withdrawn, but not before Margaret had seen an odd expression, of mingled pleasure and pain, flicker across Julian Freyton's normally forbidding countenance, as though the gesture—and the words which had accompanied it—had been unexpected and had caught him momentarily off his guard. He shook his head and said something, the glass partition cutting off the sound of his voice, and the Marquesa answered him with a laugh, evidently more amused than offended by his remark. The surgeon's expression relaxed.

Margaret turned in her seat to gaze rigidly ahead of her once more, feeling as if, without intending to do anything of the kind, she had been eavesdropping, although she had heard nothing of what had been said.

The big car gathered speed as they left Barcelona and the traffic cleared. In front of them, starkly silhouetted against the skyline, the great rocky peaks of a mountain range rose steeply, fading to purple and blue in the distance. To their right, Margaret caught occasional glimpses of the sea, of flat, golden beaches and shimmering water, bordered by white-walled villas, some half hidden behind a sheltering belt of pine trees.

They took a sharp left-hand turn at a road junction and began to climb, the road narrowing as it curved upwards into the foothills. The houses became fewer, and when occasionally they drove through a village, there were no pretty, creeper-grown villas, only the drab dwelling places of obviously far-from-well-off peasants. Goats and hens clustered about them, scraggy and dispirited, searching in the dust for food, and now and then a laden donkey plodded wearily back from the fields, its owner seated well back on its bony rump, apparently sleeping.

Ramón kept a finger on the horn button as they approached each village, seldom lifting it until they had negotiated the single, narrow street and, passing the village shrine, found themselves once again on the open road. He drove fast and expertly, silent now, since evidently he considered that there was nothing here of note to point out to his passenger. Margaret would have liked to ask him several questions about the places through which they passed, but, deterred by his silence, she did not do so.

They continued to climb. As the mountains came nearer, Margaret saw that they were bare and craggy—great, precipitous cliffs, devoid of vegetation, which culminated in weird, fantastically shaped pinnacles, resembling no others she had ever seen before. She wondered, inexplicably chilled by the vista opening up in front of her, whether the Marquesa de Fontera's chateau lay among these harsh, inhospitable peaks and why, if it did, Mr Freyton had spoken of its beauty so enthusiastically. But then, almost without warning, they turned off, taking a narrower road still, which left the mountains on their left and, several miles ahead of them, appeared to lose itself in a forest of pine trees.

Ramón said, breaking the silence, 'Over there, *señorita*, is the Benedictine Monastery of Montserrat, of which surely you must have heard.'

'Oh yes, of course I have,' Margaret assured him. 'Many pilgrims go there, don't they, to visit the Basilica of the Black Virgin?'

The chauffeur nodded. 'Many,' he agreed, 'throughout the ages, and the monks give hospitality to all comers, no matter what their race or religion. It is a big place, although you cannot realise it from so far away, and there is a village there, with an hotel and any number of guest houses, where pilgrims are accommodated. Many young couples go there on their honeymoon, to ask the blessing of the Virgin of Montserrat on their marriage and on their children.'

He talked on and, as she listened, Margaret looked back over her shoulder at the dimly seen outlines of the monastery, seeming at that distance to be a part of the tall cliff at whose foot it was built.

'Doña Luisa,' Ramón went on, his tone suddenly grave, 'went there after her marriage to my late master, Don José.'

Something about his voice as he said this, some hint of bitterness in his words, caused Margaret to glance at him in mute question. But he did not attempt to explain his meaning to her, only shrugged his immaculately uniformed shoulders and asked unexpectedly, 'This doctor who comes with you, *señorita*—he is a very skilled and clever surgeon, is he not?'

'Mr Freyton? Yes, of course he is. He is a consultant at the hospital where I was trained.'

'You think that he will cure the poor little one, Don Felipe?'

Margaret hesitated. Training and a natural, instinctive caution made her reluctant to offer any positive reassurance, certainly until she had seen her new patient and Mr Freyton had examined him. So she said, noncommittally, 'Mr Freyton is a most experienced surgeon. He will do all that is possible for the little boy.'

The chauffeur sighed. His concern for his employer's crippled son was evident in both eyes and voice as he said softly, 'I shall go myself to the Basilica to ask the holy Virgin's blessing on him, *señorita*. Although—' He broke off, eyeing Margaret covertly.

'Well?' Margaret prompted, 'Although—?'

Ramón shrugged again. 'It is of no matter,' he evaded. 'I was about to say only that it is a very sad thing when the heir to so great a name as that of Fontera should be a weak and helpless cripple. My late master, now—ah, there was a man, *señorita*!'

'You . . . admired him?'

'Who could fail to admire him? He was everything that was fine, a man of noble spirit and great courage— an aristocrat, in every sense of the word. Tall and of splendid physique, a strong man, *señorita*, and yet he was gentle and kindly, generous to a fault. His whole household was heartbroken when he died. I do not think that Doña Leandra will ever fully recover from the loss of Don José as long as she lives.'

'Doña Leandra?' Margaret questioned. 'But surely you mean . . .' Involuntarily she glanced behind her, to where the Marquesa sat, still deep in conversation with Mr Freyton.

The chauffeur's lips compressed. 'Doña Leandra,' he returned, 'was the mother of Don José, *señorita*. For a mother, the loss of her eldest son must always be a terrible thing, but for her—' He lifted his hands from the wheel, in a gesture of strange finality. 'It was the end of her life, too, I think. Certainly I have not seen her smile since the day when the news was brought to her. That is why it is so important that little Don Felipe should be cured. Doña Leandra does not like to think that a cripple should be Marqués de Fontera, when there are others who are better fitted to succeed to Don José's title.'

For a moment Margaret was a trifle puzzled. Then her face cleared. Ramón had spoken of the late Marqués as Doña Leandra's eldest son: obviously, there must be other sons.

'You mean that Don José had brothers, younger than himself?' she suggested.

Ramón changed gear, as the road twisted into a series

of descending hair-pin bends. 'Yes, *señorita*,' he confirmed. 'He had two—Don Carlos and Don Jaime. Don Jaime is serving in the Army, but you will meet Don Carlos. It is he who administers the estate, until little Don Felipe comes of age.'

His voice was flat and expressionless, betraying nothing of his feelings, but Margaret sensed that, for some reason, Ramón did not extend to the unknown Don Carlos the wholehearted admiration he had expressed for the elder brother. Probably, she thought, the chauffeur was typical of the retainers of most old and noble Spanish families in the fierce loyalty he gave to those whom he served personally. From the little he had said, he appeared to be devoted to the boy, Don Felipe, who was now Marqués de Fontera and the head of the family, and to the boy's grandmother, Doña Leandra.

She wondered whether that devotion applied also to the present Marquesa and, remembering Ramón's tightly compressed lips and the constraint in his manner when the Marquesa's name had been mentioned, decided that it did not. The Marquesa was his master's widow, but she was an American, a foreigner, completely alien to the family into which she had married and to its servants. Perhaps Ramón resented her on this account, or perhaps, although he had not said so, he blamed her for the fact that her son was a cripple. And yet how could he? He seemed well educated: his command of English was excellent, his knowledge of Barcelona and its history far beyond what might have been expected of one in his position. Surely it was unlikely for a man of his attainments to subscribe to peasant superstition? But his tone had been a very odd one when he had told her of the Marquesa's visit to the Basilica at Montserrat, following her marriage to his master. What had he said? 'Doña Luisa went there, after her marriage to Don José . . .' implying, of course, that she had gone in order that she might ask a blessing on her marriage and on the children she and Don José would have. On the poor little Don

Felipe, who had developed spondylitis and was a cripple . . .

Ramón said, abruptly breaking into Margaret's thoughts, 'Señorita, we are almost there. Look, there are the gates.'

He pointed, and, at a bend in the road ahead of them, a pair of intricately fashioned, wrought-iron gates came into view, hung between pillars of stone and set in a high, moss-grown stone wall. The chauffeur sounded an imperious fanfare on the horn, and as they approached, the gates swung open, as if directed by an invisible hand. Only when they swept through at undiminished speed did Margaret catch sight of the man who had opened them, a white-haired, wizened old creature, who stood, cap in hand, bowing as the car glided past him.

An avenue, lined with tall, shady trees, led from the gateway to the home of the de Fonteras. To the right, a small stream flowed placidly through well-kept parkland, but to the left stretched the pine forest of which Julian Freyton had told her, Margaret recalled, on the eve of their departure from London. It was a vast, far-reaching sea of dark green, covering the rising ground for as far as the eye could discern, and for the first moment or two after catching sight of it, Margaret's attention was distracted by its vastness from the destination they were approaching so rapidly. Ramón's gesture drew her gaze to it, his 'Is it not beautiful, *señorita*?' evoking from her an answering sigh of wonder and delight.

Julian Freyton had spoken of a fairy-tale castle in the mountains, and this description was, she realised, no exaggeration.

The ancient stronghold of the de Fonteras rose in a cluster of walls and turrets and tiled roof-tops from the slope of the hillside on which it stood, the dark backcloth of the pine trees behind it causing every detail to stand out in sharp relief. Bathed in the golden glow of the setting sun, it looked indeed like some fairy palace, more imagined than real, and so beautiful that her first startled glimpse of it brought a lump to Margaret's throat.

She had little or no knowledge of architecture, but it was evident, even to her untutored eyes, that parts of the building were medieval. They were remarkably well preserved, and if they had been added to or reconstructed, whoever had caused the work to be done had been at considerable pains to ensure that the new buildings should blend indistinguishably with the old.

A Renaissance gateway, with the de Fontera arms carved in stone, led into a square, paved courtyard, with a fountain playing in its centre, overlooked on three sides by the windows of the palace. The fourth side, Margaret noticed, was shuttered, and, from its air of disuse, appeared no longer habitable. The other three, in striking contrast, looked very much lived in and well cared for, the shutters gleaming with fresh paint. Incongruously, a telephone cable ran from the top of the gateway to somewhere in the interior and a rakishly low-slung sports car, its hood up, was parked just beneath it, in the shadow of the massive arch. Apart from these signs of modernity, she felt that she was entering another, half-forgotten world and, had a knight in armour come galloping across the courtyard or a troubadour emerged on to the balcony at the top of the arch, to strum melodiously on his lute, she would have experienced little surprise, Margaret thought. It was the presence of the sports car which, in these surroundings, seemed to require an explanation.

They crossed the courtyard and Ramón slid the black limousine smoothly to a halt in front of a flight of worn stone steps on the far side of the fountain. Before he could leave the driving seat, a door at the head of the steps swung ponderously open and a liveried manservant came hurrying down to meet them. Two maids, in sober black dresses, hovered by the door, waiting until they should be summoned. Behind them, through the half-open door, Margaret could just make out a spacious, shadowed hall, with a staircase curving gracefully from it to the upper floors.

The manservant opened the rear door of the car, an arm out to assist the Marquesa to alight. Mr Freyton followed her, but, forestalling the servant, he came round to Margaret's side and said, as she climbed out to stand facing him, 'Well, did you find the drive interesting, Sister Hay?'

'Oh yes, indeed I did!' She wasn't aware of her shining eyes or even of the excitement her voice betrayed, but Julian Freyton smiled. 'And you're evidently as enchanted by this place as I am?' he suggested. His smile widened when she nodded her assent. 'It's a museum piece, of course—and as fascinating inside as it looks from here, I can promise you. The pictures alone are worth a fortune . . . but you'll have time to explore its wonders during your stay. Now I expect you're tired, aren't you, and longing as much as I am for a hot bath and a cup of tea?'

'I am,' Margaret admitted, 'especially for the tea.' She was more tired than she had realised and made no demur when, taking her arm lightly, Julian Freyton urged her towards the steps.

'Well, everything's laid on, the Marquesa assures me—even the tea. She says she knows that all British hospital nurses require tea at regular and frequent intervals to keep them going, so don't disillusion her, will you, Sister? Because I gather she's detailed a special maid to attend to it and to see that you have everything else you need.'

'That's very kind of her,' Margaret said, forcing a warm note into her voice. 'If the maid is anything like as entertaining as the Marquesa's chauffeur, I shall be in good hands.' She turned to thank Ramón, who was unloading luggage from the boot of the car. 'He is a walking encyclopaedia of knowledge, Mr Freyton. I learnt a great deal about Barcelona during our drive here.'

'Did you? Excellent, Sister.' If he was aware of any hint of sarcasm in her words, Julian Freyton gave no sign of it. Apparently he was perfectly satisfied to leave her to the company of servants, Margaret thought bitterly, so long as her supply of tea wasn't in doubt. She added, her tone formal now,

'At what time do you intend to examine the patient, Mr Freyton? You'd like me to be there, wouldn't you, and to tidy him up before you see him?'

He frowned, glancing at his watch. 'Let's say in a couple of hours, shall we? I'll send word to you when I'm ready. His own doctor is coming here for a consultation and he'll be bringing me the X-rays and other reports before I see the boy. I'll want time to study them. You have a rest, Sister. After your late night and that riotous party at the Nurses' Home'—his smile returned, faintly tinged with malice—'I'm sure you oughtn't to go on duty the minute you arrive. Why not wait until tomorrow morning?'

'I should like to meet my patient,' Margaret told him, resenting the allusion to her late night, 'if you don't mind, Mr Freyton.'

Julian Freyton shrugged indifferently. 'Very well, if you insist. Far be it from me to keep you from your patient, Sister Hay—I just thought you might be tired, that's all. I know I am, and I probably got more sleep last night than you did.' Reaching the hall, he released his light grasp of her arm. 'Ah, there's the Marquesa, and I see that Carlos is with her. He is her late husband's brother, Don Carlos de Fontera . . . come and be introduced to him, won't you?'

Margaret followed him, conscious of a certain curiosity. In the dim light of the hall, with its shuttered windows, she could not at first see much of the tall, dark-haired man who stood with his back towards her, talking to Louise de Fontera at the foot of the staircase.

But when, hearing the sound of their approaching footsteps, he turned to face them expectantly, she saw that he was quite young and exceptionally good-looking, a slim, well-built man of perhaps twenty-eight or thirty, with very bright, intelligent brown eyes. He and the fair-haired, beautifully dressed Marquesa made a strikingly handsome couple, standing there side by side, yet Margaret—for no reason that she could possibly have explained—received the impression that, if they had not actually been quarrelling a moment or so before, then they had come perilously near to doing so. The hostility between them was a living thing, reflected in both their faces and shining in their eyes.

It faded so swiftly when Julian Freyton introduced her that she wondered if she could have imagined it. Carlos de Fontera gave her a charming smile, bending politely over her hand and asking, with apparent concern, whether she had had a good journey and whether or not she was tired.

'You must allow me to get you a drink, *señorita*. It is a long drive from Barcelona, over these dusty roads of ours—I expect you are parched, are you not? Why—'

The Marquesa interrupted him, her tone cool and uninterested, as it had been at the airport. 'It's all been taken care of, Carlos. Sister Hay will go to her room and I have arranged for Pilar to look after her. She will want to unpack and change into uniform—won't you, Sister Hay?' Without waiting for Margaret's assent, she motioned to one of the hovering, black-frocked maids and gave her instructions, in rapid, incomprehensible Spanish. The maid, a small, elderly woman, nodded dutifully. She had Margaret's suitcase in one hand, her small dressing-case, with its airline labels, in the other, and was obviously waiting to escort her to her room. As Margaret moved to follow her up the long, curving staircase, Louise de Fontera said in English, 'Ask Pilar for anything you want, Miss Hay—she speaks English quite well and will take you to my son's room, when you are ready to go to him. I imagine you'd like to have a meal a little earlier than we have ours—the Spanish custom is to dine late, as perhaps you know. So Pilar will serve dinner to you in your own room, whenever you ask for it.'

She smiled faintly, in dismissal, and Margaret, her cheeks scarlet, followed the small, stooping figure of Pilar to the top of the staircase. She was, she realised, to be treated as a kind of superior servant by the autocratic Marquesa. There was to be no meal in the dining room, with the de Fontera family, for her—only to Julian Freyton was this courtesy to be extended. Louise de Fontera had effectively countered her young brother-in-law's attempt to show her the kind of welcome she had expected to be given. By thus putting her so firmly in her place, the Marquesa had set an unbridgeable gulf between them, emphasising the difference in Margaret's social position and her own, making it clear that she did not consider a nurse, even a British State Registered nurse, her equal.

She was here, Margaret reminded herself a trifle bitterly, to do a job. She hadn't come as a guest, was not to be treated as one, even though she had sacrificed her holiday in order to care for the Marquesa's son in this emergency. And Mr Freyton, who was the one who had demanded the sacrifice of her, was apparently quite prepared to sit back and allow this grudging hospitality to be offered to her by his friend, the Marquesa, whom—when he had talked of her in London—he had insisted that Margaret could not fail to like. He . . .

Pilar, pausing at the end of a long, picture-hung gallery, turned, beaming, as she indicated the door beside her.

'These,' she announced, in heavily accented English, 'are the rooms which Doña Luisa has had prepared for the *señorita*.' She set down one of the cases and opened the door, standing aside to allow Margaret to precede her. 'Please, will the *señorita* not go in and see if all is as she wishes?'

Margaret thanked her and went in, some of her resentment fading as she saw the size and luxury of her new quarters. The Marquesa's hospitality was not grudging, so far as her rooms were concerned, and, if most of her leisure was to be spent here, at least it would be in extremely pleasant surroundings. The sitting room was large and beautifully furnished, with its own balcony overlooking the courtyard and a desk, set in the window, on which were piled a number of very new-looking American and British papers and magazines. The bedroom, leading off it, contained a magnificent, carved four-poster bed, which looked like an antique and was probably priceless, with a portable radio on the table beside it, a sofa and two wing chairs at its foot, covered in rose brocade, which matched the bed cover and hangings. Beyond, separated by a communicating door, was a bathroom, tiled in cream, with a carpeted floor.

Pilar waited, watching anxiously until Margaret had completed her inspection of the rooms. Then with pathetic eagerness she pointed to the tray, set with lovely, egg-shell-thin china, on the table in the centre of the sitting room.

'Tea for the *señorita*,' she said.

'Thank you,' Margaret answered gratefully. She sat down, feeling suddenly very ready for the tea which the Marquesa had so thoughtfully provided. Pilar fussed round her while she drank it. 'It is all right?' she enquired, her brown face set in worried lines, her eyes searching Margaret's. 'It is how the *señorita* likes it . . . *English* tea?' On Margaret's assuring her that it was, her brow cleared. 'Then I go to prepare the bath and to unpack for the *señorita*, yes? A bath, after a long journey, is—how do you say? Refreshing, not? The *señorita* will feel less tired, when she has bathed herself, I think.'

Margaret did, indeed, feel much less weary and dispirited when she emerged from the steam-filled bathroom, half an hour later. Her uniform, freshly pressed, was laid out on the bed. As she dressed, her confidence returned. Somehow, with the donning of the familiar blue uniform, she felt as if she were returning to normal, and, as she tied her Sister's bows neatly beneath her chin and surveyed her image in the full-length mirror on the wardrobe door, she found herself smiling back at it.

'You're being pretty idiotic,' she informed the face in the mirror, 'and probably you're imagining slights which were never intended. In any case, this is private nursing, you're not a St Ninian's Sister now, so you might as well get used to it. *And* to having your meals served to you up here. After the operation, you'll be so busy, you'll be glad if you're allowed to eat alone and you know it!'

Her own face smiled back at her ruefully and, her temper restored, Margaret went briskly back to the sitting room and rang the bell for Pilar.

A strange maid, little more than a child and obviously very nervous and in awe of her, answered the ring.

'Yes?' she said, and waited, twisting her hands, her eyes avoiding Margaret's.

'I should like you to take me to my patient's room,' Margaret told her, adding, as the girl looked mystified, 'To Don Felipe. He is ill and I am to look after him.'

Understanding at last, the child nodded solemnly.

'Please,' she invited, 'if the *señorita* will come, it is this way.'

They emerged side by side into the corridor and the little maid quickened her pace, pointing ahead of her to a winding corridor, leading away from the main hall. This, too, was hung with paintings, but so dimly lit that Margaret could make out little more than the shape of the frames. They traversed it, her guide skipping along so quickly that Margaret was hard put to it to keep up with her.

Finally, she halted in front of a heavy wooden door, tapped on it softly and then, evidently hearing some sound from within which did not reach Margaret's ears, nodded and pointed to the door.

'Please, you go in, *señorita*. It is all right.'

She bobbed a quaint little half-curtsey and made off in the direction from which they had come, her slippered feet making no sound on the thickly carpeted floor.

Margaret, a trifle puzzled by the out-of-the-way position of the sickroom, pushed open the door. The moment she entered the room, she realised that her guide had misdirected her. In place of the small, sick boy she had expected to see, there was a white-haired woman, seated in an armchair in front of the window. She was dressed in black and wore a *mantilla*, which gave her an extraordinary dignity, and, as Margaret started to back away, with a murmured apology, the woman turned, motioning her to remain where she was.

'I'm sorry,' Margaret began, 'I must have made a mistake, I—'

'No.' The voice was quiet and controlled, the English perfect. "You have made no mistake, *señorita*. I ordered you to be brought here because I wish to speak to you before you go to my grandson. I wish to . . .' There was a studied pause, while two piercing dark eyes searched her face. Then a thin white hand clasped hers and the voice became urgent, '*Señorita*, I wish to warn you. I *must* warn you, before you undertake the care of my grandson. Please, will you not sit down and hear what I have to say? It will not take long.'

Margaret sat down obediently in the chair on the other side of the window and waited, her heart absurdly quickening its beat.

'I am Doña Leandra de Fontera,' the white-haired woman announced. She lowered her voice. 'Perhaps they have told you of me?'

CHAPTER FOUR

'WELL?' prompted the white-haired Doña Leandra, her tone that of one accustomed to instant obedience. 'Have they told you of me, *señorita*?'

Margaret hesitated, uncertain of how to reply to this question without giving offence. To admit that the chauffeur, Ramón, had been the only person who had mentioned Doña Leandra's existence would be to imply that she listened to the gossip of servants; on the other hand, to admit that no one else had said a word about her patient's grandmother might be equally unwise and possibly hurtful.

Finally she said, trying not to sound too evasive, 'I have, of course, heard of you, Doña Leandra. But I have only just arrived here and I am finding it all a little confusing. I was on my way to my patient's room and—'

Doña Leandra cut her short with an imperious wave of her hand. She looked relieved, Margaret noticed, and an unmistakable gleam of triumph lit the piercing dark eyes as she said, 'My daughter-in-law, the widow of my son, the late Marqués de Fontera, likes to imagine that *she* is in control of this household, *señorita*. In fact, this is not so, and it is from me, please, that you will take your orders, when it is necessary. I wish personally to supervise the treatment of my grandson, you understand.'

'I . . . understand, *señora*. But I am responsible to Mr Freyton, the surgeon who will operate on your grandson. He has brought me with him from London—' Margaret began. Again and still more imperiously, she was interrupted.

'But naturally,' Doña Leandra assured her, 'so far as Don Felipe's medical treatment is concerned, the surgeon is in full charge and I shall not dream of interfering with him in any way. But there are other ways in which I must interfere and'—she lowered her voice—, 'things of which I must warn you, Miss . . . your name is Hay, is it not?'

'Yes,' Margaret replied, her bewilderment increasing. Again this strange old lady spoke of warning her and she wondered, casting a covert glance at the thin, lined face so close to her own, whether Doña Leandra de Fontera ought to be taken seriously or not. Ramón had spoken of her grief at her son's death. It was possible and, indeed, seemed likely that the poor soul's mind had been affected by her tragic loss, so that she imagined dangers which did not exist. Her manner was odd, her expression frankly alarming in its sudden vindictiveness as she said, in a harsh whisper, 'Miss Hay, you must guard my grandson well. You must never leave him alone, even for a moment, once the operation is performed and he lies helpless in the plaster cast. There are those, you must understand, who do not wish that he should be cured. Trust no one, Miss Hay. Not even'—her eyes flashed fire—'not even his mother! Have I made myself quite clear to you?'

Margaret decided that it was time she put an end to this strange interview. Convinced now that the unfortunate old woman was raving, she rose determinedly to her feet and stood looking down at her, a slim and dignified figure in her impeccably starched uniform.

'Doña Leandra, you must excuse me, please. I know my duty to my patient and I shall do it, to the best of my ability and in accordance with Mr Freyton's instructions. Your grandson will not be neglected, I give you my word, so long as I am nursing him. But it will not rest with me who visits his sickroom. Even if it did, I could not possibly exclude his mother. When a child is ill, it is his mother he wants and needs most, and experience has taught me, during my hospital training, that a child whose mother visits him regularly makes the best progress.'

The light flickered and died in the dark, unhappy eyes. Doña Leandra said bitterly, 'If you will not heed my warning you will regret it, *señorita*. I am not asking you to exclude anyone from Don Felipe's sickroom—I am asking only that you will not leave him alone with any visitor while he is helpless and, perhaps, semi-conscious and therefore unable to cry out. Do you imagine that it was easy for me to ask this of you, a stranger?'

'No,' Margaret conceded reluctantly, 'I don't suppose it was, Doña Leandra. But all the same—'

'It was necessary,' the old lady put in, 'or I should not have humbled myself as I have, believe me!'

Feeling unexpectedly sorry for her, Margaret said gently, 'Don't worry about the little boy, madame. I promise that I will take great care of him. Until he regains full consciousness after the operation, I shall be with him. He won't be left alone.'

Doña Leandra appeared, at last, to be satisfied. Her head, in the graceful *mantilla*, bowed in dismissal and she said, smiling now, 'Thank you, Miss Hay. I am sure that I may rely on you implicitly. You do not look to me the type to break your word, and I am glad that I have had the opportunity to meet and talk to you. Ring the bell, as you go out, will you, please, and someone will come to escort you to my grandson's room.'

As if the effort she had made had exhausted her, she lay back in the tall chair and closed her eyes. She was asleep—or pretending to be—by the time Margaret, having rung the bell, reached the door and slipped through it into the dimly lit corridor.

No one came in response to her summons. She waited, peering about her in the dimness, trying to recall in which direction she might hope to find her own suite, when the sound of hurrying footsteps, ascending a flight of uncarpeted stone stairs to her left, brought her head round. The footsteps were a woman's, quick and light, and thinking that they heralded the belated return of the little maidservant who had brought her here, Margaret went to the head of the staircase and called softly.

The footsteps halted and a gasp of astonishment came from below. Then the Marquesa mounted the last few steps, to stand for an instant transfixed, staring at Margaret as if she could scarcely believe the evidence of her own eyes. Surprise was swiftly succeeded by dismay and finally by annoyance. She asked, her voice controlled but far from friendly, 'What in the world are you doing here, Miss Hay? This part of the house is occupied by my mother-in-law, Doña Leandra de Fontera.'

'I know,' Margaret answered, resenting the other's tone. 'I came because I was sent for and—'

'Sent for? Who sent for you, for any sake?'

'Doña Leandra sent her maid to fetch me. Otherwise, of course, I should not have come.'

The Marquesa looked as if she were about to question the truth of this, but, controlling herself with almost visible difficulty, she asked sharply, 'For what reason did she wish to see you, Miss Hay?' And then, when Margaret didn't at once reply, 'You did see her, didn't you?'

'Yes, but only for a few minutes. I think—' Margaret broke off. It was obvious that she could not repeat what Doña Leandra had said without betraying a confidence and, in any case, the last person to whom she dare mention the warning she had received was her patient's mother, so she ended noncommittally, 'I think that she was anxious to satisfy herself as to my ability to take proper care of my new patient.'

'Was that what she told you?'

'More or less, yes. It was rather difficult to make out exactly what she did want. Donña Leandra is old, isn't she? And—'

'And mad,' the Marquesa stated bluntly. 'You realised that, of course? You must have done, with your training. She doesn't know what she is saying half the time. My husband's death was a great shock to her and she's never really recovered from it. At the time, her mind was unhinged and she had to receive treatment.

She's very much better now, but she still isn't normal. That was why I was upset at finding you here. We try to keep this wing of the house private, so that she's not disturbed.'

'I'm very sorry,' Margaret apologised, but without contrition, 'I didn't know anything about it, you see.' It was odd that, now that she had received confirmation of her suspicions concerning Doña Leandra's state of mind, she felt less inclined than she had before to believe that the old lady was insane. A little confused, perhaps, even senile, but not, she was certain, really mad, as the Marquesa had suggested. Although, of course, what she had said about not leaving little Don Felipe alone with his mother was patently absurd. She glanced covertly at the Marquesa and was again struck, as she had been at the airport, by the hardness that was visible beneath the beauty of her face. Her mouth was lovely, but there was a ruthless twist to it and, at this moment, although the anger in them had faded, her eyes were ruthless, too—ruthless and ice-cold.

As if sensing Margaret's gaze on her, she relaxed and smiled, and this wrought so swift a change in her appearance that the younger girl found herself wondering whether she had imagined some, at least, of the repellent ruthlessness. Smiling, the American Marquesa was really beautiful, and when she said warmly, 'Why, of course, how could you have known?' Margaret began to feel more than a little guilty. To cover her momentary confusion, she looked at her watch and suggested diffidently that perhaps it was time she made the acquaintance of her new patient.

'I'll take you to him right away, Sister,' the Marquesa promised. 'He's longing to meet you and you'll find him very easy to understand, as he speaks English perfectly—better, really, than he speaks Spanish. *I* saw to that.' She gestured towards the corridor on her right. 'This way. I expect you are feeling rather lost, aren't you?'

'I am,' Margaret confessed. 'This is such a vast place, isn't it?'

'It's a mausoleum,' the Marquesa said bitterly. She led the way down the long, picture-lined corridor, her high-heeled shoes making a sharp clicking sound on the polished parquet as she walked. 'A mausoleum,' she repeated, 'and it all belongs, alas, to my son!'

Puzzled by her evident bitterness, as much as by her words, Margaret said nothing. After a moment's silence, the Marquesa began to tell her about the boy, giving details of his illness with an almost clinical detachment that added to her bewilderment.

'Felipe has become progressively worse,' she said, her voice flat and expressionless. 'Now he can scarcely move at all and is entirely confined to his bed, which inevitably, of course, is having a very bad effect on him. He suffers a good deal, but, although he doesn't complain, he quickly becomes bored and loses heart, and there is very little one can do to help him. At one time, he was a voracious reader—now he won't open a book and he will lie for hours, with his eyes closed, not sleeping but refusing to speak to anyone. I'm afraid you are going to find him difficult to deal with, Miss Hay. Although with the prospect of the operation and the new hope it has given him, he has been less depressed the last few days. And, as I told you, he is longing to meet you—yours will be a new face and he sees so few strangers that your coming has been something to look forward to.'

'I hope I shan't prove a disappointment to him,' Margaret said, feeling that some sort of reply was expected of her. She added, as an afterthought, 'Don Felipe knows Mr Freyton, of course, doesn't he? I mean, they have met before and—'

'Naturally they met when I took my son to his consulting rooms in Harley Street,' the Marquesa put in coldly. 'If that constitutes knowing Mr Freyton, then yes, he does, Miss Hay.' She opened a door, leading to another corridor, and motioned Margaret to precede her. 'My son's room is opposite. It overlooks the rose garden and I chose it so that he could have absolute quiet. The room in which the operation is to be performed is next door.'

'Next door?' Margaret could not hide her shocked astonishment. 'Do you mean that the operation will be done *here*, madame?'

'Why not?' challenged Louise de Fontera.

'I . . . don't know. Somehow it did not occur to me that—well, I suppose I took it for granted that Mr Freyton would insist on a hospital or—or a nursing home in the city, in Barcelona.'

'Mr Freyton is perfectly satisfied with the arrangements I have made, Miss Hay—all of which have been supervised by our family doctor, who will assist him. We employ a large staff here and it is much more convenient to have my son in this house afterwards. He faces a long convalescence, as you must be aware, and having constantly to drive into Barcelona to visit him would take up more time than I have to spare. I have, of course, arranged for a nurse to relieve you—she will be arriving here this evening and I shall leave you to settle your hours on and off duty between you.'

'I . . . see.' The Marquesa's tone was one which brooked no argument and Margaret did not argue. If Mr Freyton was satisfied, there was, of course, no more to be said. The operation was not one in which, as a rule, there was any danger to the patient's life, but in every surgical procedure there remained the risk of emergencies and complications, with which hospitals were equipped to deal and private houses, however well staffed, were not. But obviously Julian Freyton, as an experienced and conscientious surgeon, would have taken all this into account when agreeing to the arrangements which had been made, and, if the room chosen to serve as an operating theatre had been prepared under the supervision of a qualified medical man, then presumably it would have been properly prepared. Whoever was to give the anaesthetic would no doubt come equipped for any emergency which might arise and he, too, would be a qualified doctor, Margaret supposed. So . . .

'Perhaps,' the Marquesa suggested icily, 'you would like to see the operating room for yourself, Miss Hay?'

She crossed the landing and, stony-faced, opened the door immediately facing her. Margaret, in response to her impatient gesture, came to stand beside her, looking into the room. It had been stripped bare of its normal furnishings and hung with spotless white sheets; an operating table, of the latest type, occupied the centre of the room and above it a shadowless theatre lamp, also apparently of the latest type, was suspended from the ceiling. Two tables, both on castors and shrouded with more of the spotless linen sheets, had been provided for instruments, and some of the anaesthetist's equipment already stood at one end of the operating table.

'There is a bathroom next door,' Louise de Fontera announced carelessly, 'and at some time this evening they will be bringing an electric steriliser from Barcelona, which they will install wherever you find most convenient. Dr Garcia is seeing to the necessary instruments, of course.' She paused, watching Margaret's face, and then asked, with dangerous calm. 'Well? Can you find any fault with my arrangements?'

Margaret had to confess that she could not, yet, in spite of this, she was worried. All her training had taught her that a hospital was the proper place for the performance of surgical operations, and when Barcelona, a modern city with up-to-date hospitals, was so close at hand, it seemed not only a needless risk to take but also a quite unnecessary expense to insist on performing this operation here for the sole purpose, it seemed, of avoiding inconvenience for the patient's mother. Almost against her will, Doña Leandra's words came back to her and they were still going round and round in her head when the Marquesa, with a cold, 'This way, please,' led the way out, closing the door firmly behind her.

She said, 'My son's room is here, Miss Hay,' and

opened the second door. To Margaret's surprise, she did not herself come in. 'You can introduce yourself,' she stated flatly, 'for, as I told you, my son speaks perfect English. I shall probably come later, with Mr Feyton and Dr García, when they have finished their consultation.'

Margaret went in obediently. The room, she saw, had, like the one next to it, been stripped of its normal furniture and prepared as a sickroom. The plain, white-enamelled hospital bed stood by the window and there was a glass-topped table beside it, on which a tray had been set out, with thermometer, feeding-cup and a selection of medicine glasses. Screens stood in readiness at the foot of the bed; there was an armchair, with a shaded lamp at its back, and a temperature chart, clipped to a board, hung from the bed rail.

An elderly woman, in the plain black garb of a housemaid, was seated at the bedside. She rose as Margaret entered and bobbed her a quaint little curtsey, gesturing, a finger to her lips, to the still figure on the bed.

'He is . . . sleeping now,' she whispered, in carefully accented English and smiling, indicated the chair she had vacated. 'Please, you will sit down? I fetch tea for you.'

Before Margaret could tell her that tea was the last thing she wanted just then, the woman had vanished, leaving her alone with the sleeping boy. She did not sit down but stood, her brows meeting in an anxious pucker, to study him as he slept.

Don Felipe de Fontera was a good-looking boy, despite his wan, sickroom pallor and over-thin face. His lashes, thick and luxuriant as a girl's, flickered as she bent over him and Margaret guessed that he was feigning sleep, in order that he, in turn, might study her.

She submitted to his scrutiny, at the same time continuing her own. The boy, she realised, had not inherited his mother's fair colouring. He was dark—as, no doubt, his father must have been—and his hair, worn long and in need of brushing, was as thick and luxuriant as his lashes but very straight. He did not look his age, for he was small and under-developed, but there were lines etched deeply about his mouth and eyes which pain had set there, making his face seem old and tired. Margaret's heart felt heavy as she looked at him. He had so much, this poor child—an old and honoured name, vast estates, more money than most people dreamed of, and yet . . . she sighed. He looked unloved and strangely uncared-for, and it was evident that he had endured a great deal of suffering in his short, unhappy life.

She put out a hand, pityingly, to smooth the ruffled hair and the boy's eyes opened.

'Good evening,' he said politely. 'Are you the English nurse?'

'Yes, Don Felipe.'

'Won't you sit down?' the boy invited. He had a slight American accent, which accorded oddly with his grave manner and typically Spanish courtesy. Margaret looked about her for his toilet things and, finding a brush and comb, crossed to the dressing table to fetch them.

'I think,' she said, 'that if you don't mind, Don Felipe, I should like to tidy you up a bit before the doctors come to see you.'

'Very well,' he agreed indifferently, 'if you wish.'

Margaret set to work. She re-made his bed, shocked and distressed to see how thin his small, pain-racked body was and with what difficulty he moved. She fetched a bowl of water and gently washed his face and hands, before attending to his neglected hair. There was no time now to give him a blanket bath or change his pyjamas for clean ones, but she did what she could, one eye on her watch. The boy submitted phlegmatically to her ministrations, but, when she had done, he said, a note of pleased surprise in his harsh young voice, 'You are very gentle. You did not hurt me at all, as María does when she tries to move me. And you did not tug my hair, either, when you combed it.' He made a wry face. 'I feel very comfortable now.'

'I'm glad,' Margaret told him, with sincerity.

'What is your name?' Felipe asked.

'It's Hay, Sister Margaret Hay.'

'Margaret?' His nose wrinkled. 'In Spanish it is Margarita. I do not have to call you Sister Hay, do I? I may call you Sister Margarita, perhaps?'

'Certainly you may, Don Felipe.'

He grinned boyishly. 'Then you must call me Felipe. So we shall be friends.'

'Very well,' Margaret agreed gravely. The old woman who had been sitting at the bedside returned, beaming, with a tray of tea. She set it down on a table, which she drew up at the window, and waved a hand to it invitingly.

'For the *señorita*—English tea!'

Margaret thanked her. Crossing to the table, she glanced enquiringly at her patient. 'Would you like to drink a cup of English tea with me, Felipe?'

The boy nodded. 'It is refreshing, isn't it? They say it is.'

'Try it and see. *I* think it is.' An arm around his shoulders, she helped him to raise his head and held the spout of the feeding-cup to his lips. The boy drank slowly and appreciatively, pausing once to smile at her. 'It is not bad, though I think I prefer coffee.'

Margaret lowered him gently back on to his pillows.

'Perhaps you'll develop a taste for it, if I'm with you for long.'

His dark brows met in a frown. 'How long will you stay with me, Sister Margarita?'

'Until you are fully recovered from your operation.'

He asked her about the operation, brows still furrowed. His questions were intelligent and he asked them without fear, listening quietly as she replied to them.

'You think I shall walk again, when it is done?'

'Oh yes, I'm sure you will, when the plaster is taken off. But you will have to be patient, Felipe, because it will take time, you know.'

'Yes, I know that. It is a pity'—his lips tightened—

'that my mother would not agree to my having the operation last year, when we were in England. Mr Freyton wanted me to have it then. If my mother had let me, it would all have been over by now, wouldn't it, and I should be walking instead of lying here like this?'

'Well, you are going to have it now. The time will pass. It won't be long before we have you walking again,' Margaret offered consolingly. She set down her teacup, hearing the sound of voices in the corridor outside. 'Here come the doctors, I think. They—' She broke off, as Felipe put out a thin hand to clutch at hers. 'What is it? You're not afraid, are you? Mr Freyton only wants to examine you.'

The thin fingers clasped hers tightly. 'It will hurt,' Felipe whispered apprehensively. 'Stay with me, won't you? Don't go away, Sister Margarita, please!'

'Of course I won't,' Margaret promised. She rose to her feet as Julian Freyton came in, preceded by a tall, bearded man of about sixty whom she assumed was the family physician, Dr García.

Mr Freyton introduced her and then, turning to Felipe, he said compassionately, 'Well, Felipe, we meet again. How are you, old man?'

The boy's answer was muffled, but Margaret was struck by the expression on Mr Freyton's normally cold, forbidding countenance. It was unexpectedly tender, as if, for some reason she could not have explained, this boy held the key to his heart. She gently freed her hand from Felipe's, but not before the surgeon had noticed the movement and included her in his smile.

'So you've made friends with each other, you two? I'm glad—I was hoping you would.'

Felipe smiled back. 'She is nice, your Sister Margarita, sir. And very beautiful, too, do you not think so?'

Margaret was aware of Mr Freyton's eyes on her face, briefly, appraisingly. He opened his mouth to reply to the boy's question, but Dr García forestalled him.

'Indeed, Felipe,' he said with heavy gallantry, 'you are

fortunate in having the most beautiful nurse it has been my good fortune to meet in the entire course of my career! That English colouring . . . it is beyond comparison, it is unique.' He bowed in Margaret's direction.

Julian Freyton said, with all his usual asperity, 'Well, Sister, let's get on, shall we? I should like to examine your patient, if you please.'

Margaret stepped to the bedside and, with practised efficiency, drew back the clothes. 'Just lie quite still, Felipe,' she whispered. 'Mr Freyton won't hurt you, I promise.'

Felipe's teeth closed fiercely over his lower lip but he waited bravely, offering no protest.

The examination was a lengthy one, but Julian Freyton was gentleness itself, his skilled hands palpating and probing with a delicacy that won Margaret's instant, though silent approval. He said little as he worked, watched intently by the Spanish physician. Occasionally their eyes met and a mute message was exchanged, and then, when it was over and Margaret was settling her patient, the two men left the room to continue their consultation out of Felipe's hearing.

Mr Freyton returned, ten minutes later, alone. He said brusquely, 'I'd like a word with you, Sister, please. Come next door, would you?'

He led the way into the improvised operating theatre, motioning Margaret to close the door after her. Then, with a gesture which expressed both annoyance and resignation, he indicated the room and its contents.

'You've seen this, I believe?'

'Yes,' Margaret admitted, 'the Marquesa showed it to me, Mr Freyton.'

'When I agreed to perform this operation,' the surgeon went on irritably, 'it was on the understanding that I should be given the facilities of a private nursing home in Barcelona. I don't approve of this arrangement at all, but unfortunately I shall have to put up with it, unless I'm to offend both the Marquesa and my Spanish colleague. Dr García has gone to an enormous amount of trouble to fit up an operating theatre here and, while it isn't by any means ideal, it is, I suppose, adequate. If I insist on a nursing home there will be complications and delays, so I've agreed very reluctantly and we shall operate tomorrow morning at nine o'clock. I'll want these instruments prepared, Sister . . .' He indicated them with a jerk of his dark head and went on to give her careful details of all he wanted done.

Margaret listened attentively. He issued instructions for the patient's pre-medication and added, his tone a trifle less irritable than it had been, 'It's going to mean an early start for you, I'm afraid, but that can't be helped. You'd better go off duty now and get as much rest as you can, while you can. Dr García is arranging for two of his own nurses to assist you. One will take over night duty and remain here with you, to nurse the boy during his convalescence, the other will only come for the operation. You understand that you're in charge, don't you?'

'Yes, Mr Freyton, I understand.'

'Good.' He turned away, making for the door. Holding it for her, he asked suddenly, 'You're managing all right, aren't you?'

'Yes, very well, thank you, sir.'

'And you like the boy?'

'Oh, yes.' Margaret's eyes lit up. 'Very much indeed.'

'Poor little devil,' Mr Freyton said, as much to himself as to her. Then, with a brisk nod, he left her, striding off down the dimly lit corridor without a backward glance. Margaret stifled a sigh and returned to the sickroom.

It was after nine o'clock when she finished, however. The two nurses whom Dr García had sent arrived at seven. The senior, a buxom, dark-eyed girl called Carmela Riardos, took over the care of Felipe, leaving Margaret free to work in the improvised theatre with the other. Nurse Riardos spoke English with reasonable fluency, if with a strong accent, but her colleague neither spoke nor understood it, which added considerably to the time they took to get the theatre ready.

But at last it was done and, with the installation of the steriliser, Margaret was satisfied that everything that could be prepared in readiness for tomorrow's operation had been attended to and nothing forgotten. She felt suddenly very tired, and after a final word with Nurse Riardos and a peep at the sleeping Felipe, she set off in search of her own room, finding it with less difficulty than she had anticipated.

A tray, with her evening meal set on it, stood on the table in her sitting room, the main course, a fish dish of some kind, with rice, being kept warm on a small spirit lamp, which Pilar had evidently lit some time before, for it was burning very low. Margaret drew up a chair and attempted to do justice to the ample provision made for her, but the food tasted oily and, after a few mouthfuls, she pushed her plate away, contenting herself with a peach, which was delicious, and a cup of very strong, lukewarm black coffee.

Pilar came in as she was drinking it and clicked her tongue disapprovingly at the sight of the untouched plate.

'The food is not good?' she enquired anxiously.

'Oh yes, it's excellent. I'm just not hungry, I'm afraid, Pilar. Or else I'm too tired to eat.' Margaret spoke apologetically. 'It's not your fault.'

The maid regarded her with a sympathetic smile. Crossing to the window, she threw back the shutters, admitting a welcome breath of cool night air. 'It's very lovely out of doors now,' she suggested. 'Perhaps if the *señorita* were to go sit five-ten minutes in the *patio*, she would feel more hungry, not?'

Margaret followed her, to stand looking down into the shadowy, moonlit *patio*. It was deserted, the fountain playing its soft, tinkling music to the indifferent stars and it looked so cool and enticing that she decided to follow the maid's advice. She picked up her cloak and, slipping it over her shoulders, descended the wide, curving main staircase to the hall. Facing her was the door by which she had entered the house that afternoon and, to her left, standing ajar, a second door which appeared to lead to the *patio* she had seen from her bedroom window.

With a moment's hesitation, to get her bearings, Margaret made for it, only to halt in the doorway with a stifled exclamation. The door led—not, as she had imagined, to the *patio*—but to a balcony raised several feet above it, overlooking the fountain. It was in darkness, but moonlight streamed in, outlining in sharp and revealing silhouette the two figures standing, locked in a passionate embrace, beside the wrought-iron railings of the balcony.

The woman had her back to the door, but the fair, beautifully dressed hair and the slender, lovely body were equally unmistakable and Margaret bit her lip to suppress a startled cry as she recognised the Marquesa.

The man who held her so passionately in his arms was tall and dark. His face was in deep shadow and hidden from her, but Margaret guessed who he was and, for some quite inexplicable reason, felt tears come to prick at her eyes as she turned to grope her way blindly back, across the deserted hall, to the foot of the staircase.

She did not know why she was so shocked. But, when she regained her own room a few minutes later, she was trembling, and the face she glimpsed, reflected back to her from the gilt-framed mirror on her bedroom wall, was white and bitter in its disillusionment. It didn't do, of course, she reminded herself, to set a man up on a pedestal and imagine that, because he was a fine surgeon with an immaculate reputation, he was incapable of behaving as a lesser man might in certain circumstances.

But was Mr Freyton's conduct really unprofessional, if she thought about it? He was unmarried, the Marquesa a widow, and, even if she happened to be the mother of his patient, there was nothing in the medical code of ethics to say that he might not make love to her, if both of them wanted it, simply because he had come here in order to operate on her son. Judging by what he had told her in the airliner on the way here, he had been in love with Louise de Fontera for a long time, years before she had married Felipe's father, and he was probably still in love with her. He might even intend to make her his wife, so therefore . . . Margaret turned away, catching her breath.

He had every right to behave as he had, but none to reproach and criticise her for her own conduct, where David was concerned—none at all.

Julian Freyton was a man, as other men were, and, in her eyes at least, he no longer occupied the exalted pedestal on which his professional attainments had once demanded that she set him. As a surgeon, he still had her loyalty and her implicit obedience, but as a man, she was seeing him through newly opened eyes, as a human being.

Strangely and quite illogically, she found this new image of him at once disappointing and hurtful and, as she undressed and got into bed, an odd little prayer went up from her heart.

To her own surprise, it was for Felipe that she prayed.

CHAPTER FIVE

MARGARET was up and ready for duty by six o'clock next morning.

Nurse Riardos rose from her chair at the patient's bedside when the English girl entered his room and, smiling, she gestured to the boy's small, calm face and said, with evident satisfaction, 'He sleeps, Sister Hay. All night long, undisturbed by fears, he has slept. It is well, is it not?'

'Indeed it is,' Margaret agreed. She glanced automatically at the chart and then, removing her cuffs, she laid them down on the dressing-table. 'Mr Freyton told me that he would operate at nine, so there's no need to disturb Don Felipe yet. I shall go and see to things in the operating theatre now, I think, but I will be back in time to give the patient his pre-medication.'

Carmela Riardos inclined her shapely dark head in acquiescence. 'He was asking for you,' she said. 'Last night, before he would consent to sleep, he made me to promise that you would be with him this morning, before he must go for his operation. He seems very much to love and trust you already, Sister Hay . . . and that also is well, is it not? To win the trust of one's patients, especially when they are children, is not always easy, in my experience. But you have done this so quickly that I am filled with admiration for you.'

'Thank you,' Margaret acknowledged, colouring faintly at the girl's directness. But she felt oddly pleased and touched by the compliment and, as she worked away methodically in the improvised theatre, the memory of last night's disquiet began gradually to fade from her mind. She had no anxiety for Felipe now. However Mr Freyton might behave off duty, in the theatre he was completely and utterly to be relied upon, a surgeon of proven ability, whose skill could not be questioned and whose integrity was beyond doubt. In her mind, as she busied herself with the instruments he would use, the image of the man was replaced by the more familiar image of the surgeon, back once again on his pedestal. So much so that when, at a little after seven-thirty, he appeared in order to see for himself how her preparations were progressing, she greeted him quite normally, and it didn't enter her head to make any reference whatsoever to the scene she had witnessed on the balcony the previous evening.

He was brisk and businesslike, but his smile, when he expressed himself satisfied with what she had done, was warmer than any smile he had ever bestowed on her in the months when they had worked together at St Ninian's.

'You've worked like a Trojan, Sister Hay. I must confess, I feel a lot happier about operating in these conditions than I did yesterday—thanks entirely to your efforts. But what about Dr García's two nurses? I know one of them is on duty with the patient, but what about the other? Surely it's about time she showed up, isn't it?'

Margaret glanced at her watch. 'I told her to report to me at eight, Mr Freyton. It's not that yet, is it?'

'No,' he confirmed, frowning, 'it's not. Have they laid on a meal for you, by the way, or have you had it?'

'I had coffee and rolls when I was called.'

His frown deepened. 'A Continental breakfast? Good heavens, that's not enough. I've ordered bacon and eggs and I expect to get it, too. Why don't you join me? You've done all you can in here and you've got a long and tiring day in front of you.' He took her arm, propelling her firmly in the direction of the door. 'Come on, Sister. There's no reason on earth why, in addition to working yourself to death, you should starve yourself as well, and there's plenty of time.'

He led her, unresisting, to the landing, and then, his

hand still gripping her elbow, down the long, curving staircase to the hall. Seeing a manservant, he issued a low-voiced order in fluent Spanish and, when the man bowed and went off to obey it, gestured towards the door leading to the balcony, through which Margaret had inadvertently blundered the previous evening.

'Here, I think, don't you? It's cool and rather pleasant and looks out on to the *patio*. We had dinner here last night.'

Taken off guard, Margaret hesitated. Then, the hot, embarrassed colour flooding her cheeks, she endeavoured to excuse herself. 'I'm sorry, Mr Freyton, but I think I'd rather not have breakfast with you, if you don't mind. Not . . . not there on that balcony. María will serve it in my room, if I ask her to, and I'm sure it would be better if she did.'

'But good heavens!' Julian Freyton stared at her in exasperation. 'I've ordered breakfast for you—didn't you hear me? If you're worrying about offending against Spanish conventions, you needn't, I assure you—no one's going to think a thing about it. They all know we're British, and in any case, even in Spain, it's considered perfectly proper for a man and a woman to eat breakfast together when they're members of the same household.'

'Yes, I—I know. But all the same . . .' Margaret broke off, unable to explain her reluctance to accompany him to the small, shaded balcony where, in the moonlight, she had seen the two silhouetted figures locked so passionately and ardently in each other's arms a few short hours before. Had he forgotten, she wondered . . . or hadn't he realised that she had seen him there? She had made no sound, perhaps neither he nor the Marquesa had heard her, perhaps neither suspected that an intruder had stumbled upon their secret and had unwittingly been present during their moment of intimacy. Certainly Mr Freyton's expression betrayed no consciousness of guilt; it was one of annoyance and controlled impatience, but nothing more.

She said, freeing her arm from his light grasp, 'The Marquesa made it quite clear to me that she wished me to have my meals in my own room, Mr Freyton. I think, in the circumstances, I'd prefer to do so, if you'll excuse me.'

'You're being quite absurd,' Julian Freyton informed her coldly, 'but have it your own way, of course. I'll tell them to send your breakfast up to you when it comes, if that's what you want. But I shall speak to Louise de Fontera about this—you probably misunderstood what she said about your meals. I imagine she meant only to have them served to you upstairs when you were on duty with Felipe, because it would be more convenient for you. She's the soul of courtesy and one of the most hospitable people I know, so I can't believe that she intended to ostracise you, Sister Hay. However . . .' He shrugged and let her go without further argument.

In the privacy of her own room, Margaret studied her flushed cheeks and angry eyes in the gilt-framed mirror and echoed Julian Freyton's accusation against herself.

She *was* being absurd, of course—quite stupidly and childishly absurd. She would do well to pull herself together and remember for what purpose she had come here. In a little over an hour's time, they would be wheeling Felipe de Fontera into the theatre, and all personal feelings must be forgotten then, subordinated to his interests, which, for the next few days, would be the only ones to matter to any of them.

A soft tap on the door heralded María with her breakfast tray. Margaret thanked her and sat down at the table in the window. She ate quickly, with one eye on her watch, and as soon as she had finished, made her way back to the theatre, where she found Dr García's second nurse already at work. Having explained by signs what she wanted her to do and satisfied herself that the other girl had understood exactly what she meant, Margaret set up a hypodermic tray and took it to her patient's room. She had her hand on the door handle when it opened and the Marquesa de Fontera emerged, to halt in the doorway, eyeing her with unconcealed hostility.

'So you've come at last, Miss Hay,' she stated, her tone as hostile and disapproving as the look in her eyes. 'My son has been asking for you very anxiously.'

Margaret indicated the tray she was carrying. 'I am just going to give your son his pre-operative injection, madame,' she answered politely, somewhat at a loss to understand the other's evident annoyance. It did not occur to her to explain that she had, in fact, been on duty since six o'clock, for she could not imagine that the Marquesa should think otherwise, until the older woman said coldly, 'Well, don't let me delay you, then. You've been fortunate enough to gain my son's confidence, but I should scarcely have thought that to keep him waiting all this time was a good thing.'

She pushed open the door and hurried off down the corridor, without giving Margaret time to defend herself against the implied reproof.

In the sickroom, Nurse Riardos was reading aloud to Felipe. She broke off in mid-sentence, to smile at her British colleague in relief. 'I am glad you are here, Sister,' she confessed, with a warning glance in the direction of the listening boy. 'Don Felipe has been asking where you were.'

'Has he? Well, I'm here, Felipe.' Margaret set down her tray and approached the bedside, her voice gentle and reassuring. Felipe's small, pale face relaxed at the sight of her and, as she bent over him, his hand came out, shyly, to touch hers.

'Then you *are* real, Sister Margarita,' he said, in a croaking whisper. 'I didn't dream you in my sleep.'

'Of course I'm real!' Margaret's fingers tightened warmly about his thin, bony ones. 'There, that feels solid enough, doesn't it?'

'Yes,' the boy admitted, but he still sounded troubled. Margaret slipped into the chair beside him, still retaining her clasp of his hand. 'What is the matter, Felipe?' she asked him pityingly. 'Has something upset you?'

He shook his head, but two large tears forced their way from beneath his long, dark lashes. 'No,' he denied, 'nothing has upset me.'

'You're not afraid of the operation? I promise you, it will not hurt. You won't know anything about it, because I'm going to give you an injection, and in a little while you will fall fast asleep. When you wake up, it will all be over.'

'I know that. Nurse Riardos has said so.'

Margaret reached for her syringe, but Nurse Riardos, with a murmured, 'Permit me, Sister,' took it from her and deftly filled it from the ampoule which lay ready in the kidney dish beside it. She repeated the dosage, tested the hypodermic by squirting a minute portion of its contents into the air and then leant forward to swab the skin of the boy's arm. Margaret took the syringe from her.

'Are you ready, Felipe?' she asked gently. 'It will only be a tiny prick, nothing more.'

'Wait,' the boy pleaded, 'wait, Sister Margarita! Tell me again, please'—his eyes, dark and haunted, met hers trustingly—'tell me again that this operation I am to have will cure me and make me walk again?'

Margaret exchanged a glance with Nurse Riardos, who sighed and murmured something in Spanish under her breath. She added, when it was obvious that Margaret did not understand, 'His mother warned him that he must not expect too much, Sister Hay.'

'But that's . . .' Margaret began, and broke off, biting her lip in an effort to still its indignant quivering. To Felipe she said, with complete sincerity, 'Believe me, Felipe dear, you *will* be cured. I give you my word you will. It will take a little time and you must be patient, but in a few months you'll be walking and running about just as if you'd never been ill. When the plaster is taken off, your back will be quite straight again, I promise it will.'

He believed her. The fear went out of his face and his smile returned, heartwarming in its gallantry. He held up his thin arm. 'Give me the injection now. I am ready.'

Margaret gave it, with the swift skill of experience. She sat with him until she saw his eyes close and then got to her feet, motioning to Nurse Riardos to join her. They prepared him together, working in silence, and then the Spanish girl said, 'You will want to go and scrub up now, will you not, Sister? Leave him with me. I will bring him into the operating room when they are ready.'

'Thank you,' Margaret acknowledged. She was grateful to Carmela Riardos for her restraint, glad that she had said no more about the boy's mother and the warning she had offered, with such needless cruelty, a little while before. Perhaps it hadn't been intentional cruelty, even if its effect had been cruel. In any case, it did no good to discuss these things: a good nurse didn't gossip about her patients or about the behaviour of her patients' relatives, at a time like this. She simply did her job, to the best of her ability, and said nothing, since it wasn't for her to criticise.

At the door of the sickroom, Margaret paused for a moment, after closing it behind her, making a conscious effort to bring her thoughts under control. The tall figure of a man, standing waiting at the end of the corridor, caught her eye and, thinking that it might be the anaesthetist, she moved towards him, only to halt when he turned and she saw that it was Carlos de Fontera, the Marquesa's brother-in-law.

'Ah, good morning, *señorita*.' His voice was lowered, its tone subdued, but he seemed pleased to see her, and as he came to stand looking down at her, Margaret realised that Felipe bore a very strong resemblance to him, and, for some reason which she could not have explained, she found this reassuring. She returned his greeting quietly and he said, gesturing to the door of the room she had just left, 'How is the child? Is it possible, do you think, for me to see him? I want only to tell him that I am thinking of him and praying that all will go well with him today.'

'I'm sorry, Don Carlos. You can, of course, peep through the door at him, if you wish, but he is asleep now.' Margaret made to open the door, but he stopped her with a shake of the head.

'No, no, I will not disturb him if he is sleeping. I have left it too late with my good wishes, which I regret. There is someone with him, of course?'

'Nurse Riardos is with him, Don Carlos.'

'I see.' His eyes searched her face, as if seeking in it some clue to her feelings. Finally he said, a note of mistrust in his deep, pleasant voice. 'Will it succeed, do you imagine, this operation?'

'I'm quite certain it will,' Margaret stated positively.

'His mother has doubts, now that it has come to the point.'

'Has she?' Careful not to betray any indignation, Margaret met his gaze quite frankly. 'I do not think she need have any doubts, Don Carlos. I hope, if you can, that you will persuade her of this. Mr Freyton is a very fine surgeon, and I have seen other cases like Don Felipe's, on which he has operated with excellent results.'

'Have you?' His smile returned. 'Then thank God for Mr Freyton! It is not right that the heir to the de Fonteras should be a cripple, is it?'

'It is not right that any child should suffer as little Don Felipe has,' Margaret returned crisply.

Don Carlos shrugged. 'As you say, *señorita*. But it is particularly unfortunate in my nephew's case, is it not?'

Margaret did not contest his statement. After a few more questions, he asked her if she had everything she wanted, and when she assured him that she had, he bowed to her gravely and took his leave. She watched him out of sight, brows furrowed, puzzled by his attitude and wondering what it meant. Then, with a quick glance at her watch, she returned to the theatre, to forget him almost instantly, since now there were other, more urgent claims on her attention.

Everything went quite smoothly. She was scrubbed up and setting out instruments when the anaesthetist made his appearance. Like Dr García, he was elderly and he spoke English. When he had put on his gown and mask, the two surgeons came in, talking together in low voices as they crossed to the basins side by side. Mr Freyton did not glance at her and made no acknowledgment of her presence, but she heard his voice above the sound of running water, describing the operation in precise technical terms to his Spanish colleague.

'We'll soon know, of course . . . a V-shaped osteotomy on each side from the inter-laminar space to the intervertebral foramen. This will allow hyperextension of the back and the resulting lumbarlordosis compensates for the dorsal and cervical kyphosis . . .'

'You think . . .' Dr García's strongly accented voice sounded guttural, 'three months' immobilisation will be enough?'

Mr Freyton's reply was lost behind his mask, but Margaret saw him nod emphatically.

'It is interesting,' Dr García observed, scrubbing his dark-skinned arms. 'I have read Alexander Law, who says, I recall, that the results are nothing short of dramatic in suitable cases . . . psychologically as well as physically. And the movements of the diaphragm are substantially increased, are they not? By reason of this . . .'

The anaesthetist interrupted them. Julian Freyton nodded again and continued with his industrious scrubbing. Over his shoulder he asked, 'You're ready, aren't you, Sister Hay?' his tone casual, as if he expected no other reply than the instant, 'Yes, sir, quite ready,' which Margaret gave him.

'Right, then . . .' He turned, thrusting his arms into the sterile gown which the young theatre nurse was holding ready for him. He added, as she went behind him to tie the tapes, 'We'll have the patient in, Dr Montez, if you please.'

Margaret's gloved hands moved among her instruments. Dr García, gowned, his own hands gloved and folded carefully in front of him, came to stand opposite her, as very slowly and with infinite gentleness Felipe was carried in and laid on the table.

He did not stir when Dr Montez adjusted his position and tilted the table and the two Spanish nurses, obeying his quietly uttered instructions, assisted him deftly.

Mr Freyton moved to Margaret's side. He waited, without impatience, for the anaesthetist's signal, and, when it came, he held out his hand. 'Scalpel, Sister, please.'

Margaret slapped it into his outstretched palm. She met his gaze then and saw that his eyes, over the top of his mask, were bright with a light she had seen in them many times before.

It spelt faith and dedication, the confidence of a skilled surgeon in his own ability to perform his appointed task. She knew, with a deep, inner conviction, that he would not fail to heal the small, twisted body committed to his hands, as he had healed others in the past. But for him, as for her, it did not matter that this child was Felipe de Fontera, the son of a grandee of Spain. He could have been any child who suffered. That, for Julian Freyton, was his importance at this moment, and Margaret was suddenly glad and thankful that it was so.

She settled quietly to her own task, watching his hands so that she might anticipate his needs, as the operation slowly progressed.

CHAPTER SIX

By evening, Felipe had returned to semi-consciousness. Mr Freyton, paying his second visit, had ordered that he be given relatively heavy sedation, and now, encased in plaster, Felipe slept, mercifully free from pain.

Margaret sat with him, doing the little that was necessary for his comfort, as the long day drew to its close. She was very tired. But her weariness sprang more, she realised, from anxiety and the responsibility she had borne than from any physical cause. For most of the afternoon, she had sat in the comfortable armchair provided for her at Felipe's bedside, waited on by Pilar and by the black-garbed old woman who had been sitting with him the previous day. They had served her lunch and had brought her trays of tea at frequent intervals. She had scarcely had to lift a finger for herself, and apart from the short time she had spent, after the operation, helping Dr García's nurse to clear up the improvised theatre, she had really been resting.

Yet, in this house, for no known reason, she found she could not relax and that even to sit in a chair was inexplicably tiring. Doña Leandra's warning, which she had told herself wasn't to be taken seriously, nevertheless haunted her constantly, and she had refused the kindly-intentioned offers of Pilar and her companion to relieve her, so that she might take an hour off duty, in her own room.

Old Doña Leandra had begged her not to leave Felipe while he was unconscious and unable to move, and, obstinately, she stuck to her post, although no one had come near the sick-room, except Mr Freyton and Dr García. The Marquesa had, it was true, opened the door a few inches and looked in, with evident reluctance, at four, when Margaret was drinking the tea which María had insisted she must have. But she had contented herself with a few whispered enquiries as to her son's condition and had made no attempt to remain with him or, indeed, to enter the room at all.

'The doctors tell me that it went very well,' she had said coolly, on leaving, and when Margaret assured her that it had, she thanked her, without warmth, and waited to hear no more. It seemed, on the face of it, rather a strange way for a mother to behave—but the Marquesa de Fontera was a strange woman. In any case—Margaret suppressed a tired yawn—her relationship with her son was her own affair. She . . .

Felipe stirred restlessly and a tiny moan escaped his parted lips.

Margaret rose at once and went to him, smoothing the ruffled hair from his face. He wasn't conscious and almost immediately was asleep again, his thin little face shuttered and remote. She checked his pulse and returned to her chair, putting out a hand to pick up the book Nurse Riardos had been reading to him, some hours before. It was, as she had feared, in Spanish and quite incomprehensible to her, so she let it fall again. She had a book and one or two magazines of her own in her room; next time she went there, she would bring them back, she decided, if only in order to while away the time. It was difficult, in the stuffy heat of the sickroom, to remain alert, if one had nothing to do and no one, except servants, to whom one could talk. But perhaps if she washed her face in cold water, it might help . . . stifling another yawn, Margaret got up again and crossed to the communicating bathroom, pushing her stiffly starched Sister's bows clear of her chin. It was absurd to feel so tired, she was used to long hours and lack of sleep, but of course, there had been yesterday's journey and the strain of her goodbye to David . . . and today had undoubtedly been a rather hectic one.

She ran water into the wash basin and took off her cap.

The feel of the ice-cold water on her hot cheeks was infinitely pleasant and refreshing. Margaret scooped up handfuls of it, letting it run through her fingers. Feeling better than she had felt all day, she took out a comb and, having done her hair, she set to work to repair her make-up. But, in the act of replacing her cap, a sudden sound in the room beyond set her pulses racing. She dropped the cap on to the bathroom floor and jerked open the door, to find herself staring into the dark eyes of Carlos de Fontera who, evidently bending over the bed a moment before, had turned, startled, at the sound of her approaching footsteps.

For one shocked second, he appeared visibly taken aback, then, recovering his composure, he accused her, smiling, of having frightened the life out of him.

'I had no idea that you were here, *señorita*,' he admitted ruefully.

'And I had no idea that *you* were,' Margaret informed him reprovingly.

'I beg your pardon, I did, as it happens, knock several times. Receiving no answer, I came in. I wanted to see how my nephew was. My mother, Doña Leandra, is anxious to be given a first-hand report on him, you see, so I promised I would obtain one if I could. How *is* Felipe, Miss Hay? I must confess'—Carlos looked down at the sleeping boy with narrowed eyes—'he does not look very well. But then I am a layman. No doubt, after a major surgical operation, all patients look as he does now?'

'Most of them do, Don Carlos.' Margaret went to the bedside. A glance sufficed to show her that Felipe was exactly as he had been before and she turned back to the visitor with more cordiality. 'Your mother may see him, if she would like to, for a few minutes. But he isn't conscious and won't know her, of course, and if you think it might upset her to see him like this—'

'I do,' Carlos said firmly. 'The boy is drugged still, isn't he? Tomorrow, when he is fully conscious and can speak to her, I will bring my mother to see him. She is devoted to him, you understand, and it would distress her to visit him now. I'll tell her'—his smile widened—'that he is . . . how do hospitals always put it? As well as can be expected. That's what you say, isn't it?'

'Yes. It's sometimes all we can say.'

'But he—Felipe is all right, I trust? He's not in any danger?'

'Oh no, none at all, Don Carlos,' Margaret told him. 'He came through the operation very well indeed.'

'And you—how are you feeling, Miss Hay? You look tired, I think.'

'I am tired,' Margaret confessed. She looked round for her cap and, retrieving it from the bathroom, was about to don it when Carlos extended a slim brown hand to take it from her.

'Tired or not, you look charming without this thing. Must you put it on? Is it essential to your care of Felipe that you wear it?'

She laughed. 'Not really, I suppose. But it's part of my uniform, and on duty I am supposed to wear it. Mr Freyton would be horrified if he came in and found me without my cap.'

Carlos sighed and relinquished the cap. He asked, as she resumed it, 'For how much longer must you remain in uniform and on duty? Have you not been working all day without respite?'

'Nurse Riardos will relieve me at eight o'clock. After that, I shall be free and—'

'Free?' he echoed quickly. 'Free to do what, if I may ask?'

'To have a hot bath and go to bed,' Margaret told him wryly.

He shook his head emphatically. 'No, you must not do that. *Dios*, a hot bath and bed, with your dinner, no doubt, served to you in your room! And you are in Spain . . . for the first time, is it not? Sister Hay, it would do you far more good, I assure you, to let me take you into

Barcelona for dinner. That would be stimulating, it would take your mind off all your problems and anxieties and give you a new lease of life. Besides, to escape from this house for a few hours . . . don't tell me that you would not like to? It would not necessarily make you late. If I promise to have you back here by midnight, will you not consider it? You would be giving me so much pleasure if you would.'

Margaret hesitated, conscious suddenly of his charm and his good looks. To dine with an escort like Carlos de Fontera, in Barcelona, would be a new experience for her, an adventure. She was tired, but her tiredness was, as she had recognised earlier, more mental than physical. Perhaps he was right and stimulation was what she needed more than rest: escape from the strained atmosphere of this vast, troubled house what she needed most of all.

She looked up at him, wondering whether he really wanted her to accept his impulsive invitation or whether, having issued it on impulse, he now regretted the fact. But he didn't appear to: the smile he gave her was eager, his dark eyes bright with admiration as he added pleadingly, 'Miss Hay, you would be doing me a great kindness if you came with me this evening. I, too, must work hard, you know. It is a long time since I have gone out purely to enjoy myself and even longer since I have taken a lovely young woman to watch *flamenco* . . . and if you have never seen it, ah . . . then that would add immeasurably to my enjoyment. Please—say you will come with me. You know the old adage about all work and no play? Well, then, does it not apply to us both? Have we not earned a few hours' freedom?'

'I think perhaps we have,' Margaret conceded. 'But—' She thought of Mr Freyton and knew that he would disapprove of her going. And there was the Marquesa, who had made it abundantly clear that she considered herself and her family on a different social plane from that occupied by a British hospital nurse. But on the other hand, after the tense little scene she had witnessed between them last night, had either of them any right to disapprove of her, if she accepted an invitation to dine with Carlos in Barcelona, or anywhere else for that matter? Since he *had* invited her, it was obvious that Carlos himself attached no social stigma to her profession. He and the Marquesa accepted Mr Freyton as a social equal, because he was a consultant surgeon, and her own father was also in Harley Street . . . her face relaxed in a smile.

'All right, Don Carlos, if you would really like me to, I'll be delighted to come.'

He bore her hand to his lips. 'That is wonderful, *señorita*! From the bottom of my heart, I am grateful to you. Till eight o'clock, then? I shall be waiting for you, as soon as you are ready, at the wheel of my car.'

He left her then and Margaret returned to her vigil, her depression gone, a feeling of eager anticipation driving out her weariness.

Nurse Riardos reported for duty at half-past seven.

'You have been working all day, Sister,' she said, her plump face wreathed in smiles, 'and must, I feel sure, be anxious to finish your duties. So I am early, which will perhaps give you time to take some fresh air in the *patio*, now that the sun has set.'

Unwilling to let her assume this, Margaret, a trifle pink, confessed that she was going to dine in Barcelona, and the Spanish girl expressed wholehearted approval. 'Ah, but I am pleased for you! You will enjoy it, you will eat our fine Spanish food and see the *flamenco* dancers, you will have such amusement. Go, Sister Margarita, do . . . you may leave everything to me with confidence. I will see that all your instructions are carried out, just as if you were here yourself.'

Margaret thanked her and, after a last look at Felipe, allowed herself to be bustled off. She bathed and changed into a gay little cocktail dress she had purchased for her holiday and was ready at ten minutes past eight.

A coat over her dress, she made her way downstairs unobserved, but as she was crossing the hall, Julian Freyton fell into step beside her.

'Going out for a breath of air, Sister Hay?' he suggested, with unusual affability. 'Do you mind if I join you?'

'No,' Margaret said, 'of course not. Only I wasn't . . . just going for a breath of air, Mr Freyton. I . . . that is, I'm going into Barcelona for dinner.'

'My dear girl!' He stared at her incredulously. 'It's thirty miles to Barcelona from here, you know, and to the best of my knowledge there are no buses. Besides, you can't go alone. I mean—'

'I know what you mean, Mr Freyton. I'm not going alone, as it happens. Don Carlos de Fontera has invited me to dine with him and he's driving me there.'

'*Carlos* is taking you?' Julian Freyton echoed, appalled. His face darkened and for an instant he looked so angry that Margaret instinctively backed away from him. Finally, however, he controlled his rage and asked coldly, 'Where's he supposed to be meeting you?'

'Outside in—in his car.'

'Right, let's go and find him, then.' Mr Freyton took her arm. Margaret jerked herself free. 'There's absolutely no need,' she said, matching his coldness, 'for you to take me to him, Mr Freyton.'

'Isn't there?' Julian Freyton challenged wearily.

'No, there isn't. I—'

He gave her a wintry smile. 'Sister Hay,' he said, not unkindly, 'you did a magnificent job today. You're a first-class nurse and I can't tell you how grateful I am. But this *is* your first visit to Spain, isn't it?—and you will allow, I feel sure that, having asked you to accompany me, it's my duty to assume responsibility for you during your stay here?'

'Yes, but there's no need for you to interfere with my private life. When I'm off duty, what I do is—is my own affair. You—'

Again he interrupted her. 'Certainly it is, and I'm not going to interfere. I'm simply coming with you, that's all. Just to make absolutely certain,' he added, with dry emphasis, 'that Carlos understands who and what you are and how you should be treated. Because I think your father would expect it of me, don't you?'

Rebelliously silent, Margaret walked with him to the waiting car. She did not look at Carlos as Julian Freyton said smoothly, 'I decided I'd like to join you, Carlos. Er . . . in view of the fact that I stand *in loco parentis* for my distinguished colleague, Sir Martin Hay, who is Sister Hay's father, I feel that he would want his daughter to be adequately chaperoned. So if you've no objection . . . ?'

'None at all, Julian,' Carlos de Fontera returned, when he had recovered from his surprise. 'It will be a pleasure to have you both.' He opened the door of his car and waved them into the rear seat. Mr Freyton, with the air of a courtier, handed Margaret in beside him.

CHAPTER SEVEN

THE drive to Barcelona was—despite a certain restraint on the part of Julian Freyton and some resentment on Margaret's own—a pleasant one.

Carlos de Fontera set himself out to play the role of host with courtesy and charm, although once or twice, when he spoke to Julian, Margaret thought that she detected a subtle mockery in his tone. But she couldn't be sure and the surgeon appeared not to notice it, so she let it pass and responded eagerly to Carlos' suggestions for the evening they were to spend together.

He drove his powerful sports car as fast as the narrow, twisting roads allowed, if not even faster, but he was so skilled and accomplished a driver that she did not experience a moment's uneasiness, trusting instinctively to his skill.

They left the mountains behind them, rejoining the coast road, and the moon came out to shed a glorious, silvery radiance over the smooth expanse of sea. The night air was fragrant with the scent of pine trees and the salt tang of sea water and fireflies danced like fairies among the dark boles of the closely growing trees. More than once, entranced by the beauty of the scene, Margaret was tempted to cry out in wonder and delight, but a glance at the face of the man seated beside her strangled the cry before it could be uttered. Julian Freyton spoke little; when he did so, it was not in praise of the scenery, to which, apparently, he was immune.

Carlos pulled up outside a telephone kiosk, as they were nearing Barcelona.

'Since we are to be a party, let us be one,' he suggested. 'If you will fogive me for five minutes, I will telephone some friends of mine and ask them to join us for dinner. It will be more amusing for you, Julian, don't you think? A threesome is . . . well, to put it mildly, a rather awkward arrangement, and I should like Sister Hay to enjoy her first evening of freedom.'

Without waiting for Julian's answer, he vanished into the kiosk and Margaret saw him, through the glass, talking volubly into the mouthpiece of the telephone, evidently having some difficulty in persuading his friends to agree, at such short notice, to fall in with his plans. But he returned, a smile curving his lips and said, as he slipped expertly behind the wheel of his car, 'It is arranged. They will join us for coffee, in about an hour's time. They cannot dine, since they have another engagement for eleven o'clock, but that fits in nicely, does it not? We shall have to leave about that time, if we are to be back by midnight—as I promised Sister Hay we should.'

'That will suit me,' Julian assured him. 'I'd prefer not to make too late a night of it, I must confess.'

'And you, Miss Hay?' Carlos asked, turning in his seat to smile at Margaret. He started the engine when she nodded. 'Good, then everyone is happy. We are going to the Casa Ibañez . . . perhaps you know it, Julian?'

Julian frowned. 'I don't think so . . . ought I to?'

'Well'—slipping deftly into gear, Carlos shrugged his slim shoulders as the car gathered speed—'it is not so much frequented by tourists as most of the restaurants which offer *flamenco* as entertainment, and the food is infinitely better. I thought my sister-in-law might have taken you there. It was a favourite eating place of my brother's.' He accelerated to skim effortlessly past a crowded *autobús*, and Julian's answer, if he gave one at all, was drowned by the roar of the racing engine. But, glancing at him sharply, Margaret thought she saw a gleam of anger light his eyes for an instant. Then it faded and he said, his voice quiet and indifferent, 'I expect we shall enjoy anywhere you choose to take us.'

The lights of Barcelona came into view at a bend in the

road and Margaret's attention was again distracted. They drove up one side of *Rambla de las Flores* ten minutes later and she peered out eagerly, surprised to see so many people about at this late hour and the flower-vendors still busy at their stalls.

'Don't they ever close?' she asked, and Carlos laughed over his shoulder. 'Not in the tourist season, *señorita*. This is one of Barcelona's most popular attractions, you know—I think that nowhere else in Spain is there anything quite like it.'

He slowed down for a traffic policeman's signal, the narrow, one-way street beside the flower market blocked for a moment as a tramcar decanted its passengers, and then, when the policeman's arm dropped, he moved forward again at snail's pace, in the wake of the swaying tram.

The restaurant he had selected wasn't far away. Carlos dropped Margaret and Julian Freyton at the door and went to park his car, bringing with him, on his return, a delightfully arranged posy of flowers which, with an amused glance in Julian's direction, he pinned to the shoulder of Margaret's dress.

'Roses,' he said, sweeping her a bow, 'for an English rose . . . to whom they do not do justice!'

In the act of thanking him, Margaret caught Julian Freyton's eye and, to her annoyance, felt herself flush. It was absurd, she told herself, as a waiter came to lead them to their table, to allow herself to be flustered by his disapproval. She hadn't asked him to come: he had invited himself and if he didn't like Carlos de Fontera to give her flowers, then he should have stayed away. She wondered why he hadn't, since he looked and obviously must be tired. Besides, there was the Marquesa . . . how would she enjoy being deserted without, so far as Margaret knew, a word of explanation? Mr Freyton had decided, on impulse, to accompany Carlos and herself to Barcelona and he had simply walked with her to the waiting car. He hadn't even left a message for the

Marquesa with one of the numerous servants, so that, in all probability, his hostess would have no idea where he was . . . might even be searching for him now and would certainly not be pleased when she found out why he had abandoned her. Unless, of course—Margaret's spirits rose, for some unaccountable reason, as the thought occurred to her that they might have quarrelled. Lovers did quarrel; she and David had, more frequently than she cared to remember, so it was conceivable that Mr Freyton had had a disagreement with his patient's mother.

The Marquesa wouldn't be difficult to disagree with and . . .

A large, double-sided menu was placed neatly in front of her by one of the trio of waiters now clustered about their table, who bowed and murmured a soft '*con su permiso, señorita*,' as he did so. Carlos leaned towards her.

'Do you wish to choose for yourself, Miss Hay? Or will you allow me to make your choice for you?'

'Oh . . . I'd like you to choose. I don't think my Spanish could cope with all this.'

He flashed her his ready, charming smile. 'You like shellfish?'

'Yes,' Margaret assented.

'They are a speciality here,' Carlos explained. He gestured to the menu. '*Zarzuela de mariscos*.' He entered into a long and wordy conference with the head waiter, conducted in rapid Spanish, and Margaret turned to look about her. The restaurant was a little more than half full and a number of couples, some of whom were evidently British and American tourists, were dancing on a floor of coloured glass in the centre of the room, to the slow, faintly sensuous music of a five-piece band.

To her astonishment, Julian Freyton, following the direction of her gaze, rose and came to stand by her chair.

'Shall we dance?' he invited gravely.

Margaret hesitated and then, in silence, gave him her hand. He led her on to the floor and took her into his arms. He danced extremely well and she found herself, almost against her better judgment, enjoying the unusual experience of being held in his embrace. After a while, to her shocked bewilderment, it became more than mere enjoyment. Her heart quickened its beat, she found her feet following his as if they had always danced together, and when, inadvertently, his chin brushed her cheek, she was conscious of an odd thrill running through her and, instinctively, she drew back.

'I'm sorry,' he offered politely, but his arms tightened about her and Margaret yielded to the swift, unexpected surge of emotion that swept over her, no longer questioning it or her own motives. She had never thought of Julian Freyton as an attractive man before, but that he was there could be singularly little doubt. Glancing covertly up at him, she saw that his dark face was relaxed and smiling, quite unlike the Julian Freyton she knew and a long way removed from the grave-faced surgeon whom she had assisted that morning. He looked younger and less forbidding, even . . . she drew in her breath sharply. Even happy, as if he were enjoying this dance as much as she was, as if . . . the music came to an end and the orchestra, their faces bored, laid down their instruments. The leader signed impatiently to a passing waiter.

'I'm afraid,' Julian Freyton said regretfully, 'that we've had our dance.' He didn't at once release her, and the expression in his eyes, as he held her for an instant longer, was such that Margaret's heart missed a beat and then began to pound in her breast, like a wild thing seeking release.

This was impossible, she thought, it couldn't have happened, she must have imagined it. She didn't even *like* Julian Freyton, had in fact actively disliked and resented him ever since his appointment to St Ninian's, and yet . . . she expelled her breath in a pent-up sigh. This dance had been enchantment, a magic moment, set aside in her memory now and never to be forgotten.

He let her go and she saw that, apart from themselves and a pair of young Americans, the dance floor was deserted, the rest of the dancers already on their way back to their tables and a waiter carrying a tray of drinks over to the band. Reddening furiously, she started back to rejoin Carlos, but Mr Freyton put out a hand to detain her. Tucking it into the crook of her elbow, he asked, smiling, 'Aren't you going to wait for me?'

'I . . . of course, Mr Freyton, I—'

'Julian,' he suggested, 'when we're off duty.'

She didn't answer him and, with a shrug, he released her arm. Cheeks flaming, Margaret returned to their table. Did he imagine, she wondered indignantly, that he could flirt with her, just when it suited him . . . and in the Marquesa's absence? As she remembered the scene on the balcony which she had unwillingly witnessed the previous evening, her indignation grew, and the fact that just for a moment or two, as she had danced with him, she had allowed herself to respond, added both to her annoyance and her humiliation.

Carlos de Fontera rose when she reached the table, holding her chair for her courteously. He took in her flushed cheeks and air of embarrassment, and a smile that was faintly tinged with malice played momentarily about his lips.

'You found the orchestra passable?' he asked.

'It was very good,' Margaret returned, and behind her Julian Freyton echoed, '*I* thought it excellent.'

'Splendid,' Carlos said. He added softly, 'I hope that I may have the pleasure of dancing to it with you in a little while, *señorita*. But now there is the cabaret, I think, and also our meal. I am most anxious that you should enjoy both.'

Margaret did her best. The food was beautifully cooked and served, but, for some reason, she had lost her appetite and could only toy with it. The cabaret began with a guitarist who played throbbing, passionate tunes that lingered hauntingly in the memory and stirred the senses, until the tension became almost unbearable and she was glad when, with a brief bow, he ended his performance and strutted off to the excited applause of his audience. He was succeeded by a troupe of *flamenco* dancers—three slim, dark-haired girls and a handsome, olive-skinned young man, in traditional costume—who stamped and pirouetted gracefully to the rhythmic clicking of castanets. Their performance won them even more enthusiastic applause than had that of the guitarist, as the tables rapidly filled, but for Margaret, although she clapped as enthusiastically as the rest, the magic of the evening had inexplicably been shattered.

She spoke little, pretending to be absorbed in the dancing, and Carlos and Julian Freyton carried on a low-voiced, desultory conversation about Spanish music in which, normally, she would have been deeply interested. Julian, rather to her surprise, appeared to be extremely knowledgeable on the subject, and several times Carlos deferred to his views, which also surprised her. Both men attempted frequently to include her in their discussion and, as the evening wore on, she became aware that Carlos was watching her with hurt bewilderment in his dark eyes.

He said, touching her hand, '*Señorita*, I do not think you are enjoying yourself, are you?'

'I am,' Margaret defended untruthfully. 'It was a wonderful dinner and I think the dancing is fascinating.'

'You do not look as if you are enjoying it, though,' he persisted. He added, lowering his voice, 'Why? Won't you tell me? Perhaps you would like to go on somewhere else? Somewhere less noisy, perhaps?'

Margaret shook her head. 'Oh no, Don Carlos, you couldn't have brought me to a place I like more. The trouble is that I'm tired, I'm afraid.'

He studied her thoughtfully and then glanced at his

watch. 'My guests will soon be here. But we need not stay long with them, if you are tired . . . although I think you will like them.' He turned to Julian. 'You remember my friends, probably—the de Gaulas, Don Pasquale and Doña Aracea? I think you met them the last time you were here.'

A guarded look came into Julian's eyes. But he inclined his head, 'Yes, I believe so, Carlos. Don't they own a country estate outside Seville, where they breed bulls for the ring?'

'Yes, that's right. The de Gaula bulls are famous. So also is the beauty of Pasquale's sister, Brigída, who is coming with them so that you may make her acquaintance.'

'So that *I* may make her acquaintance?'

'Certainly, my friend. As a connoisseur of feminine beauty, I feel certain that she will appeal to you strongly.' There was an unmistakable challenge in Carlos' voice, but Julian ignored it. He answered indifferently, 'Oh, I see. It's very good of you to go to so much trouble on my behalf, but you needn't have done so. I'm no connoisseur, and, even if I were, am I not already surrounded by feminine beauty?' His gesture took in the crowded restaurant, but his eyes, no longer guarded, rested for a long moment on Margaret's face. Dismayed by her inability to control it, Margaret again felt the warm colour rise to burn in her cheeks.

The dancers left the floor and the orchestra began to play a lilting tango. Julian got up. He said, his tone peremptory, 'A last dance, Sister Hay? I imagine that Carlos will want to wait for his friends to arrive.'

Margaret had intended to refuse if he asked her again, but he took her acceptance for granted, simply holding out his hand to her, so that she had no choice but to take it.

The glass floor was packed and it was difficult to move, but he guided her skilfully among the throng, until they emerged on to a free space at the far end. Then he said,

'Listen, Sister, these de Gaulas . . . I know them. They are very rich and they love a party—I think we ought to escape before they come. If you're tired, so am I, and we'll be here all night if we once get involved with them.'

'But didn't Don Carlos say they had a dinner engagement?' Margaret objected.

Julian laughed. 'And if they have, do you imagine that will stop them? If they're enjoying themselves, they'll simply hold their dinner party here, that's all. Spaniards as a race are unpunctual, time doesn't mean a thing to them and they are hospitable to a fault. I know, I've experienced their hospitality . . . I once spent a weekend at the de Gaulas' estate in Andalusia.' He made a wry face. 'I don't think I once got to bed before dawn.'

'Oh, I see.' Margaret's half-stifled yawn was involuntary, but seeing it, he shook his head at her. 'You've had a long and trying day and so have I. You'll probably have one tomorrow, and besides, we're not here on holiday, either of us. I'd like to get back, I must confess—if you've no objection.'

'None, Mr Freyton. But won't Don Carlos be hurt? I mean it was kind of him to ask us out and—'

'Kind?' he repeated, dark brows rising in their familiar, sceptical curve. 'Well, you can call it that, if you like. But when you know Carlos de Fontera as well as I do, I think you'll agree that "kind" is scarcely an accurate description of him. However . . . you can leave me to make our excuses, while you collect your wrap. I'll tell the doorman to get us a taxi.'

As he had when asking her to dance, he took her acceptance of his suggestion for granted. Leaving her in the foyer, he had a brief word with the uniformed doorman and then made his way back into the restaurant.

He was waiting, drumming his fingers on the table with impatience, when Margaret emerged from the cloakroom.

'Right, that's all settled, Sister, and the taxi is here.'

He gestured towards the door. Obediently, Margaret went with him, and the doorman, cap in hand, assisted her into the rear of a small red and black taxi, with a swarthy-faced driver at the wheel. Julian Freyton gave him the address of their destination and he grinned delightedly at the prospect of so lucrative a fare.

'Si, *señor*! We go at once.'

'How did Don Carlos take it?' Margaret asked, when her escort joined her in the stuffy interior of the taxi.

'Oh, he took it all right,' Julian assured her, but for some reason she couldn't fathom, he avoided her gaze as he said so and she guessed that Carlos had been more annoyed than he cared or intended to admit.

A beautiful grey and silver car, of American make, drew up outside the restaurant as their own taxi was leaving it and the surgeon said, with a shrug, 'Well, Carlos won't have to be on his own for long—those are the de Gaulas, arriving now.'

Margaret glanced back, to glimpse a small, exquisitely beautiful girl of about her own age descending from the car, in the wake of a man whose face she could not see, and then the taxi was turning into the stream of traffic, its horn hooting, and she saw no more.

'By all appearances,' Julian went on, his tone astringent, 'he's going to enjoy himself, too. Well, I wish him joy and I don't envy him. I must be getting old, don't you think?' He grinned at her, with unexpected and startling boyishness and then, leaning back, he sighed and closed his eyes. 'What,' he asked, without opening them, 'did I do to offend you after that first dance?'

Margaret sighed. She felt suddenly too tired to argue with him. If he didn't know what he had done, then she wasn't going to enlighten him. 'Nothing,' she returned flatly. 'Nothing you need bother about.'

'Oh, come now! I must have done something. Was it because I suggested that we might be on Christian name terms, when we're off duty?'

'No, of course not, Mr Frey . . . I mean, no, it wasn't.'

'Then what was it?'

'I tell you, it was nothing.'

He opened his eyes then and turned to look searchingly into hers. 'You're a strange girl, aren't you, Margaret?' he observed thoughtfully. 'A very strange girl indeed, at times. Tell me—do you dislike me or do I only imagine you do?'

Faced with so direct a question, Margaret found herself momentarily bereft of words. She didn't even know the answer to his question herself now. His nearness and the way he was looking at her set her pulses leaping wildly, and, when he put out a hand tentatively in search of hers, she weakly let him take it, conscious of a tiny thrill, like a current of electricity, running up her arm as he did so.

They sat, hand in hand, for several minutes, neither of them speaking. The taxi left the outskirts of Barcelona behind it and took the coast road and once again, the moonlit air was heady with the scent of sea and pines. The driver sang softly to himself as he drove, in a pleasant tenor, and although she could not understand the words of the song, Margaret sensed, from the passionate yearning he put into it, that he was singing them a love song. One of the age-old, haunting melodies of Spain, a gipsy song, perhaps, its origin lost in the mists of time but its sentiments as new and as real today as they had ever been.

Love didn't change, she thought, whatever else might change, and felt her throat tighten as it occurred to her suddenly that, sitting here beside him in this small, shabby taxi, she was in imminent danger of falling in love with Julian Freyton. But that was madness, it was unthinkable, after one dance and a drive in the moonlight, serenaded by a Barcelona taxi-driver, who was probably only doing it in order to earn a larger tip, at the end of the journey . . .

Julian shifted his position, coming closer to her.

'Margaret,' he prompted gently, 'you haven't

answered my question, have you?'

What could she say to him? Margaret wondered miserably. Last night, he had held Louise de Fontera in his arms and she had seen him, watched them together and had been indescribably shocked and disillusioned by what she had seen. Yet now . . .

'I don't dislike you, Mr Frey . . . Julian,' she managed at last, averting her gaze from his face. 'It's just that I—oh, I don't know.'

'Try to explain, won't you?'

'I . . . I can't. I'd rather you didn't ask me to, I—'

'Please,' he insisted, and captured her other hand, compelling her to look at him. 'This evening, when I was dancing with you, I almost believed . . .' He broke off, his mouth compressed. 'Do you remember what we talked about, during the flight over?'

'Yes,' Margaret admitted reluctantly, 'I remember.'

'We talked about David Fellowes,' Julian stated.

'Yes, I—I know.'

'You gave me to understand that it was all over, since his marriage—at any rate, so far as you were concerned.'

'Of course it was—*because* of his marriage—'

'Margaret,' he demanded urgently, 'you aren't still in love with him, are you?'

'Oh, *no!*' Margaret exclaimed, with a certainty that surprised even herself. 'I got over that a long time ago.'

'Good, I'm glad, I—' Again he didn't complete his sentence. Instead, his fingers tightening about hers, he said, 'I told you, didn't I, that I was once involved in a similar situation? It was a good many years ago, when I was young and impressionable, and I'm afraid I didn't behave very well . . . not as well as you did, looking back.' He was silent for a moment, brows knit in a frown, as if considering his next words. Finally, he went on, still frowning, 'This may come as something of a shock to you, but the girl—the woman I was in love with was Louise de Fontera.'

Margaret said nothing. But she displayed no surprise

and, watching her, he said accusingly, 'You guessed it, I suppose?'

She answered with a brief, 'Yes,' and was tempted then to tell him of the scene she had witnessed on the balcony. But he put in quickly, 'It was over for me too, a long time ago, Margaret. I hope you'll believe that.'

'Does it'—her withdrawal was unreasoned, instinctive—'does it matter whether or not I believe it?'

Bewilderment clouded his face. 'Naturally it matters.'

The taxi-driver broke off his singing. He swung his small, labouring vehicle off the flat coast road and they began to climb up into the mountains. Now, with soft reverence, he sang what sounded like a hymn. *'Rosa d'abril, Morena de la serra, de Montserrat estel . . . illuminau la catalana terra, guiau-nos cap al cel . . .'*

'That's the *Virolai*,' Julian said, unexpectedly. 'A hymn written by a monk of Montserrat in honour of the Virgin. You hear the choristers singing it in the church up there every evening.' He quoted, in a low voice, the translation, 'Rose of April, Dark One of the Mountain, Star of Montserrat . . . shed light over Catalonia, lead us up to heaven.'

'You've been there?' Margaret questioned. 'To the monastery, I mean?'

'Yes,' he confirmed, 'but that, also, was a long time ago.' Suddenly there was pain in his voice and he looked away from her towards the dark mountains, sombre and majestic in the moonlight, their jagged, rocky peaks touched to silver.

It was several minutes before he spoke again and then, prosaically, it was to talk about their patient. He appeared not to notice that she had withdrawn her hands from his clasp and made no further attempt, as they climbed steadily upwards, to recapture them.

Margaret was conscious both of relief and a contradictory disappointment, but she listened dutifully and, when he had done, said quietly, 'Very well, sir, I understand.'

'Yes, you understand exactly what is expected of you professionally, of course,' Julian conceded glumly. 'But I'm afraid'—now there was reproach in his voice—'that you neither understand nor believe *me*, Margaret. However, I suppose I've been too premature. Well—' he shrugged—'it'll come right in time, I suppose, like most things.'

The great stone pillars of the de Fonteras' entrance gate came into view, caught in the beam of the headlights. There was some delay while the old man who attended to the gates made his appearance, shuffling sleepily from his lodge, but then the wrought-iron gates swung ponderously open, the taxi-driver re-started his engine and they rattled through.

Margaret felt a wave of depression sweep over her. They were back. All too soon, she would re-enter the vast, unwelcoming house, and a wall of prejudice, built up by the Marquesa's hostility, would once again separate her from Julian Freyton.

As if he had sensed her change of mood, Julian turned in his seat to look at her, his smile a trifle strained. But again he reached for her hand and, very gently, bore it to his lips.

'Since we're in Spain . . . thank you for a delightful evening, which it was for me. I hope I didn't spoil it for you?'

'No, you didn't spoil it,' Margaret said, conscious that this was something of an understatement.

He sighed. 'I couldn't let you go alone with Carlos, Margaret.'

'Couldn't you? I *am* old enough to take care of myself, you know. You needn't imagine that I have to be . . . protected.'

'I don't imagine anything,' he retorted, with asperity. 'But I *do* know something of the situation here and I know Carlos.' His expression softened. 'There, you're tired, aren't you? We won't talk of it any more tonight, you've had more than enough to cope with and I don't suppose I've helped, although that was the intention when we set out. Anyway . . . have breakfast with me tomorrow, will you?'

Margaret nodded, without speaking. The taxi drew up outside the stone steps leading into the entrance hall and the driver, without waiting for Julian's bidding, went running up the steps to pull a resounding peal on the old-fashioned bell. He returned to bow them out of his vehicle, the bell still jangling behind him. Julian reproved him in fluent Spanish and he apologised, crestfallen.

'Go in, Margaret,' Julian suggested, 'I'll be after you as soon as I've settled with this chap. I hope to heaven he hasn't roused the entire household.'

He had, however, roused the Marquesa. Or else she had been waiting for their return . . . Margaret saw her, coming from the room leading off the *patio*, as soon as she opened the door. She started to murmur an apology, but Louise de Fontera cut her short.

'I was awake, you didn't disturb me. Is Julian with you?' Her tone was cold, but it wasn't angry.

'Yes, he's just coming. He's paying off our taxi and—'

'*Taxi?* Then you weren't with Don Carlos? I understood he was taking you out to dinner.'

Margaret was in the midst of her explanations when Julian came in. With an imperious gesture, the Marquesa dismissed her. 'You may go, Sister Hay. A flask of coffee has been sent to your room and I expect you are anxious to get to bed, are you not?' She did not wait for Margaret's assent but, turning to Julian, started to address him in a low, urgent tone, in Spanish.

He nodded and took her arm, leading her back in the direction from which she had come. At the door he turned, and his hand raised in a casual salute, bade Margaret goodnight, his tone as casual as the wave.

Feeling absurdly as if he had struck her, Margaret retreated up the long, gracefully curving staircase, hearing the door of the balcony room close as she reached the top.

She did not go at once to her room. All desire for sleep had now vanished and she decided to have a last look at Felipe before retiring. Nurse Riardos might like to share her coffee with her, perhaps; at any rate, if she carried her tray to the sickroom, she would not have to drink it alone.

She picked up the tray and, leaving her wrap on the bed, made her way quietly down the long, picture-lined corridor. At the door of the sickroom, she paused and tapped softly, expecting the night nurse to come and let her in.

But no one answered. When, setting down the tray, she opened the door herself, it was to see no sign of her Spanish colleague.

Instead, seated in the chair at the bedside, was old Doña Leandra, a *mantilla* covering her snowy hair and her embroidery on her knee. She raised a finger to her lips and gestured to the bed.

'He sleeps,' she whispered. 'Do not waken him, *señorita*, if you please.'

But Margaret, approaching the bedside, stared in growing alarm at Felipe's white, unconscious face. She dropped to her knees beside him, frantically feeling for a pulse. The boy's breathing was so faint and shallow that the bedclothes covering his chest scarcely moved.

CHAPTER EIGHT

'IF you please, Doña Leandra—' Training asserted itself and Margaret's voice held no hint of panic, but she spoke with crisp urgency, 'Will you ask Mr Freyton to come and look at Don Felipe? He is downstairs, with the Marquesa.'

The old lady stared at her, black eyes round with surprise. She said, with hauteur, 'You send *me* to deliver your mesages, *señorita*? And'—her gesture was reproving—'you wake this poor child, when he sleeps? Is not sleep what he most needs to restore him to health?'

Margaret, busy with the unconscious boy, scarcely heard her. Felipe's pulse was rapid and shallow, his respiration alarmingly slow, and she saw that—far from sleeping, as his grandmother imagined—he was in a coma, his small face deathly pale, the lips blue. She lifted one of his eyelids, then the other. The pupils had shrunk to pin-points; and she expelled her breath in a worried sigh.

His chart, together with the case-notes and Mr Freyton's written instructions, hung at the foot of the bed. She reached for the chart and saw that Nurse Riardos' last entry had been made over an hour ago. The boy's pulse had been good then, his respiration normal, and he had been given no sedatives, according to Nurse Riardos' notes, since she herself had administered one before leaving him in her Spanish colleague's care. *According to Nurse Riardos' notes* . . . but according to his symptoms, he must have been.

Margaret glanced up, astonished to see that Doña Leandra was still sitting in her chair, watching her with resentful eyes.

'Please,' she begged, 'Doña Leandra, you *must* fetch

Mr Freyton—at once, it's urgent! Felipe is very ill and I can't possibly leave him.'

'He is ill?' Doña Leandra echoed incredulously. Margaret, adjusting the oxygen mask, which was there in case of emergency, about her patient's mouth and nose, nodded emphatically. 'Yes,' she said, 'he is very ill indeed. And I can't answer for the consequences, unless you call Mr Freyton at once.'

Her words, at last, seemed to carry conviction. Doña Leandra rose and stalked to the door of the sickroom in silence. The door closed behind her and Margaret could only hope that she understood what was required of her and would deliver the message. But there was a bell behind Felipe's bed, she remembered, an electric bell which had been specially fitted to enable the nurse on duty to summon Pilar or one of the other women servants. Praying that there would be someone about to answer it, she rang it and then returned to the bedside to do what she could for the little boy.

Julian Freyton joined her a few minutes later, the Marquesa at his heels. She flashed a frightened glance at her son and demanded harshly, 'Julian, what's wrong with him, for God's sake? He looks . . . he looks as if—'

The surgeon cut her short. 'Leave him to us, Louise,' he ordered, 'but you'd better wait outside, in case I need you.' He looked at Margaret, his fingers on the boy's thin wrist, and in a few brief sentences, she told him all she knew. He nodded, tight-lipped, when she showed him the chart and then reached for his stethoscope. 'Where do you keep your drugs, Sister Hay?' His tone was formal and peremptory.

Margaret pointed to the locked drawer in which, earlier that day, she had placed the various drugs supplied by Dr García for the patient's use. 'In there, sir.'

'Locked?' he snapped, adjusting the stethoscope.

'Yes, of course. But there's only one key. I left it with Nurse Riardos when I went off duty.' She opened Felipe's pyjama top. He was encased in plaster to his armpits, the small body grotesquely stiff and immobile. Julian Freyton motioned her to stand aside. 'Check that it's still locked, would you?' he ordered, over his shoulder.

Margaret went to the drawer. It yielded instantly to her questing fingers, sliding open as she touched it, but there was no sign of the key. Wretchedly, she reported this to Mr Freyton, but he betrayed no surprise, simply asked her, his voice quite level, to check the contents against her list.

She did so, forcing herself to remain as calm as he, but, for all her efforts, her hands weren't steady. It took her only a second or two to discover that one of the ampoules of morphine was missing from its box, and a search of the drawer, conducted with swift thoroughness, failed to reveal it. She told Julian Freyton, who nodded and issued brusque instructions.

He said, as Margaret gave him the prepared hypodermic he had asked for, 'Right, we know exactly where we are, don't we? Thank God, it wasn't a large dose and we should be able to pull him through all right. But if we'd got back any later . . .' He didn't complete his sentence, but again bent over the unconscious boy, as Margaret swabbed the skin.

Neither of them spoke after that. Together they worked with silent purposefulness to avert the threatened danger, aware of how close it had come. Nurse Riardos' continued absence worried Margaret, but now wasn't the time, she knew, to ask questions—there were too many other, more important things to be done. At last, it seemed a very long time later, Felipe stirred and his eyelids flickered.

'Good,' grunted Julian, 'that's better, isn't it? I was beginning to get a little anxious, I must confess. But he's responding. We'll keep on with the oxygen for a while and I'd like to check his blood pressure too, I think . . . thanks, if you would just lift his arm for me . . . fine.'

He went deftly about his task. Watching him, Margaret noticed that there were tiny beads of perspiration on his brow and guessed how great the strain had been. She asked, when he had finished and was replacing his stethoscope in his pocket, 'Mr Freyton, had I better tell the Marquesa that Felipe's condition is improving? You told her to wait outside, if you remember, and I imagine she will be anxious to know how he is.'

Julian Freyton's expression hardened. 'By all means tell her,' he agreed, 'if she's still there. But I doubt if she will be, somehow.'

His doubts, to Margaret's shocked bewilderment, proved to be justified. Only Pilar and the old woman who sometimes helped her were in the corridor outside the sickroom, huddled together as if for comfort, both of them in their night-clothes, their hair awry.

They crossed themselves as the door of the sickroom opened and, recognising Margaret, Pilar came apprehensively to meet her. '*Señorita*,' she asked, her voice a thin, quavering whisper in the prevailing silence of the vast house, '*Señorita*, will the little one live or die?'

'He will live,' Margaret told her, and the woman seized her hand, covering it with kisses. Her thanks were voiced in her own tongue, hysterical in their relief, but she calmed herself when Margaret asked for the Marquesa.

'Doña Luisa is in her own room, *señorita*,' she answered, as if this were the logical place for Felipe's mother to be at such a time. 'I am to bring her news at once, those are her orders. She is very much upset, beside herself—she said that she could not stay here, simply waiting.'

'And Doña Leandra?' Margaret enquired. 'Will you tell her too, please? I expect she will also be worried.'

'María shall go to her,' Pilar promised. She gestured to her companion, who was watching them with the tears streaming down her lined old face, as she endeavoured to follow their conversation. 'María was nurse to little Don Felipe,' the younger maid offered, in explanation of her companion's distress. 'So she was much worried, you understand. But Doña Leandra was not worried. She was telling us that she did not believe the boy was ill at all, that you were mistaken, since she had been sitting with him for more than an hour after Señorita Riardos went away. And when I asked her if we should send for Padre López, she said that it would not be necessary because little Don Felipe was only sleeping and no one had been near him to harm him.'

Puzzled, Margaret stared at her. 'Señorita Riardos *went away*?' she echoed. 'But she was on duty, she was the night nurse, Pilar—why did she go away?'

Pilar shrugged her thin shoulders helplessly. 'I do not know, *señorita*. I know only that Ramón has driven her back to Barcelona, with all her luggage, but I did not see her go. And now, if you will please excuse me, I must take this good news of Don Felipe to Doña Luisa. She will be waiting, you understand, and will be angry with me if I do not tell her at once. I will make you tea, if you wish, when I come back.'

'No.' Margaret shook her head. 'Thank you very much, Pilar, but I still have the coffee you left for me in my room. I haven't touched it yet.'

She decided, as she returned to the sickroom, to bring the tray of coffee with her. It was in a thermos flask and no doubt Julian Freyton would be glad of a cup, if she offered him one.

He was seated in her chair at Felipe's bedside when she returned and his tired face brightened when he noticed the tray she was carrying.

'Coffee?' he said, in answer to her enquiry. 'Yes, indeed, if you've a cup to spare.' He rose, offering her the chair. 'You must be ready to drop—come on, sit down, let me deal with the coffee. This young man'—his smile in Felipe's direction was unexpectedly tender—'is going to be all right now, I think. But I'm afraid he's going to need watching pretty closely for the next few hours.'

Margaret sat down wearily. She felt limp with exhaustion but she started to pour the coffee. 'I'll stay with Felipe, Mr Freyton,' she volunteered. 'There isn't anyone else, you see. Apparently Nurse Riardos has left . . . according to the maid, Pilar, she's gone back to Barcelona, taking her things with her. You don't know why, do you?'

Julian accepted the cup of strong black coffee she had poured for him and sipped at it thirstily. 'Yes,' he admitted, 'I know why—Louise de Fontera was in the middle of telling me about it when you sent for me, as a matter of fact.' He frowned. 'It's rather an odd business. I don't know what *you* thought of Riardos—you'll know more about her work than I do—but she struck me as a well-trained, reliable nurse, I must say.'

'She was,' Margaret assured him. 'I would have trusted her in any circumstances. Besides, she's a very nice girl. I liked her and we were getting on well together.' She emptied the contents of the thermos flask into its cap, eyeing it ruefully. There was less than a tablespoon of coffee remaining and she drained it at a gulp.

Julian set down his empty cup and rose. 'I'm afraid you didn't get much, did you? Shall I ask for some more? You gave me more than my fair share, or else the flask wasn't full.' He smiled when she shook her head. 'Actually, you didn't miss much . . . I never think thermos coffee is good, and that was very bitter and far stronger than I like it. Are you sure you don't want me to order more for you . . . fresh?'

'I'm quite sure, thank you, Mr Freyton. I'll send Pilar for some later.'

'Right.' He consulted his watch. 'We'll divide the night duty between us. I'll relieve you in two hours' time and I'll get García to send for another nurse in the morning.'

'Nurse Riardos won't be coming back, then?' Margaret questioned.

'It seems unlikely.' Julian again bent over Felipe, lifting each eyelid in turn and watching the slight but regular rise and fall of his chest. 'He's come to no harm and it won't even be necessary to waken him, but—' He sighed and reached for the chart hanging at the foot of the bed, with his own instructions attached to it. He studied these for several minutes without speaking, going carefully through Nurse Riardos' report. Then he passed the chart to Margaret.

'Nurse Riardos appears from this to have done her job most efficiently,' he observed, 'and she spoke good English too, didn't she?'

'Oh yes, very good indeed.'

'You're sure she understood my instructions regarding sedation?'

'Yes, Mr Freyton, I am. I made certain of that before I left her and handed the drug key to her.'

'I imagined you would. But the fact remains that I didn't write up any morphia for Felipe, apart from his premedication this morning. Yet he was given it and—'

'But surely not by Nurse Riardos?' Margaret protested.

'She was in charge and she had the key of the drug cupboard,' Julian pointed out unanswerably.

'Yes, but all the same—' Wearily, Margaret got up and came to his side. 'I gave Felipe his last injection, before I went off duty.' She repeated the dosage. 'Nurse Riardos checked it with me and I noted it . . . here, you see?' She indicated the entry, in her own neat handwriting. 'Since his pre-medication this morning, Felipe hasn't had morphia, Mr Freyton. He's had only the drugs you ordered and they have all been noted, at the time they were given, haven't they?'

The surgeon's frown deepened. 'Yes,' he admitted, 'they have. But you know the state we found him in, don't you?' He crossed over to the drawer in which the drugs had been placed, opened it and picked up the box containing the morphine ampoules. These, Margaret knew, contained hyoscine and atropine, in addition to the morphia, and both box and ampoules were clearly marked. It wasn't possible for the drug to have been administered by mistake, least of all by a trained nurse, but, to guard against even this remote possibility, she and Nurse Riardos had listed the contents of the drawer and had kept a record of any they had removed. Julian Freyton, she saw, was checking the list. He said, holding up the box, 'There are two ampoules missing and only one accounted for—the one you used for the pre-med. this morning. Right?'

'Yes,' Margaret agreed wretchedly.

He gave her a quick, encouraging smile. 'This isn't your fault. You probably saved the boy's life by recognising what was wrong and sending for me so quickly. You mustn't blame yourself for what happened, Margaret.'

'I—I don't. It's only that I feel responsible. I ought not to have gone out, I—'

'Nonsense. You and I are both entitled to our off-duty. We left—or thought we left—competent people in charge, didn't we?' As he had in the taxi, Julian put out a hand to take hers, but now Margaret was conscious of no thrill, only an aching misery as she looked up into his face. 'Come now,' he chided her, 'it's over and our patient is quite safe.'

'Is he?' Margaret challenged. She wanted to say 'For how long?' but something held her back, and he said, patting the hand he held as if she, too, were one of his patients in need of comfort and reassurance, 'Of course he is. It wasn't a large dose, after all, was it? Admittedly, in a case like this, morphia can act as a respiratory depressant—that was why I didn't order it. But it wasn't given alone and it's extremely unlikely to have done any lasting harm. Obviously it was a mistake. Nurse Riardos—'

'You still think,' Margaret interrupted, 'that Nurse Riardos made the mistake?'

'What else can I think? She had the key.'

'But that's missing,' she reminded him.

He shrugged. 'She probably took it with her when she left.'

Margaret hesitated. 'Mr Freyton—'

'Well?'

'You said just now that you knew why she left. Will you tell me why?'

He released her hand. 'Yes, of course—there's no reason why you shouldn't know, except that it may destroy your faith in her nursing capabilities. Louise de Fontera came up and found her fast asleep. Considering this a grave dereliction of duty, Louise lectured her and, I gather, the girl resented it and was extremely insolent. People like the de Fonteras aren't accustomed to insolence, so Louise sent her packing, then and there.'

'And left old Doña Leandra to sit with her son?' Margaret put in, with more than a hint of reproach in her voice.

'Well, apparently the old lady insisted on being allowed to stay,' Julian answered mildly. 'She's devoted to Felipe, you know.'

'Yes, but she's hardly a fit person to leave in sole charge of a sick child, is she? She had no idea that anything had happened or that he was ill . . . she was sitting here sewing. I had to plead with her to go and find you. She wouldn't go at first, even when I told her it was urgent.'

His frown returned. 'Is that so? Oh, well, we'll have to look into it in the morning. Now'—he glanced at his watch and stifled a yawn—'I think it's time one of us got some sleep. I suggested your taking the first couple of hours because, as a nurse, you'll be of more immediate use to the patient than I shall, but if you'd rather do it the other way round, then I don't in the least mind. It's up to you.'

'I'll stay now,' Margaret decided, and was rewarded by the warmth of his smile.

'Thanks . . . though it isn't really fair to ask you. You must be very tired.' His smile vanished when she shook her head and he vainly attempted to stifle another yawn. 'I must confess I am! I can hardly keep my eyes open . . . another reason why you'll be more help to the patient than I could hope to be. I'm not used to sitting quietly in a chair and remaining alert. But give me a couple of hours' sleep and I'll be good for the next twelve. Even if we can't get hold of another nurse at once, I promise you, you shall sleep your head off tomorrow, Margaret.'

Margaret thanked him and went with him to the door. He gave her a few brief instructions, insisted that she must call him if she was worried about their patient and then, assuring her that he would be back to relieve her in two hours' time, he vanished down the long, shadowy corridor.

Left alone, Margaret busied herself with Felipe, removing the mask of the inhalation apparatus after a while, as Julian Freyton had ordered, and carefully checking the boy's condition. He was so much improved that she decided not to replace it and she was putting away the mask when a sharp, peremptory tap on the door heralded the arrival of the Marquesa.

She was still fully dressed and looked as soignée and beautiful as always, save for a pinched tightness about her mouth, which might have been the result of the strain she had been subjected to or which might, equally easily, have been annoyance. She greeted Margaret coolly and crossed to the bedside, to stand in silence looking down at her son.

'He is better,' she said at last, her words a statement rather than a question. When Margaret confirmed her surmise, she simply inclined her head and made to depart, without any expression of gratitude or any attempt to apologise for the absence of the nurse who should have relieved her. Instead, she offered without enthusiasm to have coffee sent, if Margaret required it, and wished her a peaceful night, taking it for granted that she would remain at her post without being asked.

Margaret was tempted, for a momemt, to contest this assumption, but she thought better of it. She was too spent and weary to argue, and in any case, she thought wryly, if she were to do so, it would probably be considered insolence by Louise de Fontera. Far better to wait until the morning when, with Julian Freyton's backing, she would insist on adequate relief being provided. Or else . . . her heart lifted at the thought. Or else she would insist that Felipe must be transferred to a hospital or nursing home in Barcelona where, if she continued to 'special' him, she could at least do so under proper conditions. Julian couldn't object to this, since obviously it would be in his patient's best interests and since, in any case, he would be leaving himself for London very soon. Margaret knew then, with chilling certainty, that whatever she had promised, it would be impossible for her to stay here, in this house, once he had gone. She couldn't and wouldn't take the responsibility for Felipe, if she had to bear it alone. She . . .

'Goodnight, Miss Hay,' Louise de Fontera said softly. She turned, her hand on the door, to look back at Margaret, and, uncannily as if she had read the English girl's thoughts, her blue eyes held a gleam of triumph as she added, 'Felipe is in your care, don't forget. I shall hold *you* responsible if any more mistakes are made.'

She slipped out of the room gracefully before Margaret, now seething with bitter resentment, could think of a suitable reply.

When she had gone, Margaret forced herself to go calmly on with her work. It was useless, she was aware, to lose her temper or even to allow Louise de Fontera's attitude to upset her. But she wondered, her mind unable to comprehend fully why it should be, how a man like Julian Freyton could ever have been in love with a woman like Louise de Fontera. And how, having once escaped from her toils, he should apparently be willing to take the risk of becoming ensnared a second time, as, it seemed, he was . . . in spite of his protestations, during the drive back from Barcelona.

And then, as she emptied the drawer of the drug cupboard of its dangerous contents, re-locking these in a second drawer and carefully pocketing the key, she found herself wondering how Nurse Riardos could possibly have made the mistake she appeared to have made. *If* she had made it. Admittedly, she had not known the Spanish girl for long, but long enough, surely, to have been able to judge the standard of her work? And that had not been careless. She was the last person, Margaret thought, either to have made a mistake or to have slept when she was on duty—she had been conscientious in the extreme. In any case . . . she crossed to the table, on which Julian had left the chart and the case-notes, and picked them up. Nurse Riardos could not have slept for long, since her notes and the entries on the chart covered the period during which she had been on duty, except for the last hour when, presumably, after her dismissal, she had been sent to her room to pack.

She sighed, replacing the chart at the foot of Felipe's bed. Julian Freyton had promised to look into the matter next day. It was a waste of time, when her brain was tired, to attempt to puzzle things out now. But they would have to *be* puzzled out. Perhaps, next time she was off duty, she could go to Barcelona and find Nurse Riardos, talk to her, ask her to explain what had happened, give her the chance to explain, which Louise de Fontera had denied her. Perhaps . . .

A second knock, hesitant this time, interrupted Margaret's thoughts. She went to the door and found old María there, with a tray, set with coffee and sandwiches. The woman thrust the tray into her hands and, dropping her an awkward little curtsey, she whispered hoarsely that the Marquesa had sent it and scurried off, like some small, frightened elderly mouse, seeking the safety of its hole.

Margaret drank the coffee gratefully, sitting in her chair at Felipe's bedside. It would, she thought, help her to ward off her weariness, keep her wakeful for the last hour of her vigil. But, contrary to her hopes, it didn't. Twice she felt her eyelids close, of their own volition; once she let her chin fall from the hand on which she had propped it. Remembering what Julian Freyton had said, about the difficulty of remaining alert while sitting quietly in a chair, she forced herself to get up and walk about the room. But it was no use. Her legs would not support her and her knees felt as if they had turned to jelly. She tried, concentrating all the will power she possessed on the simple task, to check Felipe's pulse and respiration, but half a dozen times she lost count and had to begin again.

When, eventually and after prolonged effort, she succeeded in making an accurate check, she reached for the chart to record the figures, but it slipped from her outstretched hand and, when she bent to pick it up, the room whirled about her in crazy circles, so that she was forced to return to her chair, sick and giddy.

After that, the desire for sleep became so urgent and so overpowering that she was unable to fight against it any longer. Dimly conscious of the fact that, like Nurse Riardos, she was failing in her duty, Margaret made a last, supreme effort to reach the bell behind her patient's bed. Her eyes tightly closed and heavy as lead, she groped for it in the darkness that was closing about her and felt it beneath her fingers. But it was suddenly beyond her power to ring it, and her hand slipped away, losing contact with its smooth, cool surface, and she was unable to locate it again.

She sank back into her chair, spent and defeated. The darkness descended and shut her in a swift, suffocating cloud, against which she struggled vainly to get her breath. Her last thought, as she lost consciousness, was that Julian Freyton had promised to relieve her in two hours' time and that the two hours must nearly be over. She prayed that he would not be late and groped, in the stifling blackness, for Felipe's small, thin hand lying helplessly on the coverlet, as if, by the mere action of grasping it, she might keep him safe from the danger which, she was now convinced, must threaten him.

After that, she remembered nothing more . . .

Margaret woke, to the sound of a low, persistent knocking on the door, and when she opened her eyes it was to close them again hastily, for sunlight was blazing in through the uncurtained window and the glare made her head ache unbearably.

She managed, after a while, to sit up painfully. Her limbs were stiff, her mouth unnaturally dry and parched and her headache was worse than ever. But the knocking went on and she knew that she must answer it. Rising, she glanced fearfully over to the bed, as memory slowly returned. Felipe lay, sleeping quite peacefully, just as she had left him, his colour good, his lips curved into a little half-smile, as if he were dreaming and his dream a happy one. His hand, still linked with hers, lay on the disordered sheet which covered him, as, she realised, it must have lain all night . . . and lain undisturbed, either by herself or by the intruder she had feared, in her despair, might come when she lost consciousness.

Had it been a nightmare, then? Had she imagined that despairing struggle, that frightened groping in the darkness? Had she fallen asleep, simply because, after over eighteen hours without rest, she had collapsed from sheer exhaustion? Or had the coffee that María had brought her, on the Marquesa's orders, contained a drug, a sedative so strong that she hadn't been able to resist it?

She didn't know, but, looking round for the coffee tray, she saw, to her surprise, that it had gone. Someone had come into the room then, after she had fallen asleep—unless she had imagined María and the coffee too.

The knocking continued, increasing in urgency now, and Margaret wondered why whoever was there did not simply open the door and come in. It wasn't locked, it . . . she caught her breath sharply as she noticed the key, lying half on, half under the carpet in front of the door. From its position, it looked as if it had been pushed *under* the door . . .

She freed her hand gently from Felipe's and, bracing herself, crossed the room, picked up the key and fitted it into the lock. Before turning it, she tried the door handle, but, as she had begun to suspect, the door was locked and didn't yield. She unlocked it and jerked it open, to find herself looking into Julian Freyton's concerned and astonished eyes.

'At last!' There was reproach in his voice, as well as anxiety. 'I thought I was never going to make you hear. Why in the world have you locked yourself in, Margaret?'

She didn't answer his question, but instead motioned him urgently into the room. When he had closed the door behind him, she looked at her watch and from it to his face.

'Good lord, I know,' he said, shamefacedly, before she could speak. 'Two hours, I said, didn't I? And it's after eight. I have an alarm clock and I set it for half-past three. It's a pretty powerful one and normally I wake at the first ring, but although it undoubtedly went off, I'm afraid I didn't hear it. Margaret, I'm sorry, I don't know what you must think of me, leaving you to hold the fort all night, while I slept round the clock. But I've only just woken up, I'm ashamed to say . . . and *you* must be exhausted.'

'No.' Margaret couldn't keep the note of panic from sounding in her voice. 'No, I slept too, as I . . . as I was meant to. But somebody locked the door, from the outside, I think, and then pushed the key underneath, so that I'd find it when I woke up.'

Julian stared at her, evidently puzzled by her tone. His glance went to Felipe and, with a muttered exclamation, he strode over to the bed, but a swift examination satisfied him that all was well with the boy.

'Margaret—' He turned to face her again, eyes narrowed and alert. 'What did you mean by saying that you slept as you were *meant* to? I don't understand. Are you suggesting that *I* was meant to oversleep as well?'

'I . . . I think so,' she admitted shakily.

'Why? My dear girl, *how*? Surely you're not implying that we were doped, are you? I've never heard anything so absurd!'

'Nurse Riardos slept on duty,' Margaret pointed out, 'and so did I. But I never once did it before, however tired I was—not once. A good nurse doesn't, Julian, you know that.' In her agitation, she used his Christian name and wasn't aware that she had done so. He smiled and laid his hands, gently but firmly, on her shoulders. 'You're imagining all this—or you dreamed it, my dear. Look, be reasonable—who would do such a thing? You'd gone a long time without sleep, we both had, and we're only human, after all. The operation yesterday morning took it out of us, not to mention our gallivanting with Carlos last evening. The truth of the matter is that we both reached the end of our tether and we fell asleep. I did, too, you know, and I'd every intention of relieving you, I give you my word.'

'But what about the door?' Margaret asked, still not quite satisfied. '*I* didn't lock it.'

'Are you so sure? Because you were worried—subconsciously, if you like—you probably went and locked it before you fell asleep. Or you did it *in* your sleep and dropped the key by the door. People do things like that, when they're very tired.'

'I don't remember doing it,' Margaret said, but already, in the daylight, she was beginning to be less certain, for the memories of the night were hazy and confused. She had thought that María had brought her coffee, but the tray wasn't there. Only the one she had carried in herself still stood on the table, with its empty thermos flask and the used cups. Perhaps she had imagined it or, as Julian had suggested, had dreamed a good deal of it. Subconsciously she had felt guilty, when sleep started to overcome her and—remembering Nurse Riardos—she had locked the door to prevent the Marquesa from entering the room and finding her asleep. Poor Riardos! Margaret suppressed a sigh. *She* had been dismissed—blamed for the fact that the drawer of the drug cupboard had been left unlocked and because an ampoule of morphine was missing—simply because she had fallen asleep. Yet she herself had done precisely the same thing and had been saved by a locked door, which she couldn't remember having locked.

Yet . . . the doubts returned. Surely it was too much of a coincidence that *three* of them—Julian Freyton, Nurse Riardos and herself—should all have fallen asleep, one after the other? Suppose María had also brought coffee to Nurse Riardos and Julian? Or . . . there was the thermos coffee, which he had said was bitter . . .

'Did you'—Margaret's voice was low, brittle with strain—'Julian, did you drink any coffee after you left me and went to your room? Apart from what you had from my thermos. I mean?'

'No.' Julian's denial was emphatic. 'I had a whisky and soda, if you want to know. Someone had thoughtfully provided me with a decanter and glasses, so I helped myself. I needed it, I can tell you!'

His answer didn't resolve her doubts and she started to voice them again, only to find herself cut short. 'Doña Leandra tried to warn me when I first came here . . .' she began, but he shook her gently.

'She's not to be taken seriously, Margaret—and neither are these absurd dreams of yours, you know. Forget them and go and have some breakfast and a breath of air. I'll stand in for you . . . and I've been on the telephone to Dr García, by the way. He's bringing another nurse out with him and they should both be here before you've finished breakfast. So you've nothing to worry about, honestly you haven't. The boy's in good shape and—'

'All the same,' Margaret said obstinately, 'I think he ought to be moved into a nursing home. It could be done by ambulance without upsetting him.'

'Louise won't hear of it,' Julian objected.

'She would have to if I refused to stay.'

He looked down at her frowning. 'You don't mean that?'

'Yes, I do. Julian, I'm not satisfied that Nurse Riardos made a mistake with that morphine injection last night and I don't believe she fell asleep deliberately, any more than I did. If the Marquesa won't agree to have Felipe move, then I shall leave. I mean it and I shall tell her so. I'll go back to London when—'

A sob from the bed interrupted her. Felipe cried out in a choked voice, 'Oh *no*—oh, please, Sister Margarita, you mustn't go back to London! I don't want you to leave me and I don't want to be moved anywhere. I want to stay here with you, I—I . . .' The rest of his outburst was lost in a torrent of sobs.

Margaret went to him and took him in her arms, trying to soothe him. But he would not listen to her, repeating in a frantic whisper, over and over again, 'Promise you will stay! Promise me, Sister Margarita, please . . .'

There was no resisting that pathetic plea. As she gave her promise, her gaze met Julian's over the little boy's bent head.

He said, his voice expressionless, 'I'll have a talk with Louise and see if I can persuade her to agree to what you want. But if she refuses, I should like you to stay, Margaret. This boy needs you and you'll break his heart if you desert him now. At least wait until I go, won't you?'

Margaret's hesitation was barely perceptible. But her heart sank as she realised what it meant to her to stay on in this vast, troubled house, whose menace seemed hourly to come closer . . .

CHAPTER NINE

WHEN Margaret returned from breakfast, it was to find Dr García in the sickroom, talking to Julian and Felipe.

He said, in his quaint, heavily accented English, as he bowed over her hand, 'Ah, Sister, so you are back! I am told that you were on duty with our patient not only all of yesterday but also for most of the night. You must be very anxious to meet and hand over the responsibility to your relief, are you not?'

Margaret managed a wan little smile, avoiding Julian's gaze. 'I am,' she confessed, 'although Felipe and I both had a quiet and undisturbed night, Doctor, so I'm not really as tired as I might have been. I can quite easily carry on until my relief arrives.'

'She is here,' Dr García assured her, 'and will join us as soon as she has unpacked her valise. I wonder . . .' He regarded her pensively from beneath his bushy white brows and asked unexpectedly, 'Have you ever worked with a member of a religious Order before, Sister?'

'You mean—' Margaret was a trifle taken aback. 'You mean a nun, Dr García?'

He smiled. 'Yes, that is what I mean. Sister Teresa was at one time in charge of one of our finest and most up-to-date hospitals, established by her Order in Madrid several centuries ago. Now she is old and has retired to the Convent at Vidalonia, which is ten miles from here, in the mountains. But when her nursing skill is needed, she comes, whether the patient is rich or poor. She is a wonderful nurse and the little Don Felipe will be safe with her, Sister Hay, so that you need have no further anxiety on his behalf.'

Had Julian, Margaret wondered, spoken to the Spanish doctor of her fears for Felipe's safety? She glanced at him quickly, but his expression betrayed nothing of his

119

feelings. Dr García, who evidently felt very strongly about Nurse Riardos' dismissal, was talking on, beseeching her earnestly not to judge all the members of his country's nursing profession by the actions of only one, who had proved so unreliable. Margaret guessed that he had enlisted the help of Sister Teresa, on whom he knew he could rely, in order to counteract the bad impression he feared she must have formed of Nurse Riardos. She wished that she could offer some defence of her absent colleague, but, in Julian's presence, she could do little more than say quietly that she had found the girl's work excellent when they had been on duty together.

Dr García brightened visibly. 'I am glad of that, at least, *señorita*. I have employed her on a number of my private cases and, until now, she has always given complete satisfaction. I do not understand what can have come over her to make her behave as she did to the Marquesa . . . and to mislay the key of your drug cupboard in addition! I simply do not understand it, unless of course'—he shrugged resignedly—'she is in love. Women do strange things when they are in love, do they not, *señorita*?'

Behind him, Julian murmured something which Margaret did not catch, and the two men laughed aloud. From the bed, Felipe asked anxiously when he was to see his new nurse and Dr García beamed at him and bade him have patience. Turning back to Margaret, he went on, 'There is just one little matter on which I must ask your indulgence, Sister Hay. You had arranged, I believe, that when Nurse Riardos was here, she was to be on night duty and you yourself were to take charge during the day?'

'Yes, Doctor,' Margaret confirmed, guessing what was to come. 'But if you wish to change it or if Sister Teresa would prefer to do the day duty, naturally I will fit in. I'—it was a sacrifice to make this offer, but she forced herself to make it—'I don't mind which I do.'

'It is kind of you to say so, Sister Hay. I am sure that Sister Teresa would prefer to be on duty during the daytime, although, being what she is, she would never ask it for herself. But she sleeps badly, I know, so if you really do not mind—'

Aware of Julian's eyes fixed searchingly on her face, Margaret flushed. But she said firmly, 'I will take the nights, Dr García,' and Julian, although he opened his mouth as if to speak, finally closed it again without raising any objections.

It would not, after all, be for very much longer, Margaret told herself. If Julian spoke to the Marquesa, if he insisted that Felipe was to be moved into a nursing home, then her ordeal might not last for more than a night or two. She dreaded a repetition of what she had endured the previous night, but . . . she smiled wryly, remembering. If the worst came to the worst, she could lock the door of the sickroom again, shutting herself in with Felipe until daylight. And it was an ill wind that blew nobody any good. Today, with Sister Teresa here, she could sleep to her heart's content, and later, being free in the daytime would have its advantages.

She could go into Barcelona one afternoon, to see Nurse Riardos, and when that was done, could make use of the sunny daylight hours in order to explore the city and the beaches round about—perhaps even pay a visit to Montserrat and hear the choir singing the *Virolai* in the church on the mountain top.

She was pleased, when she made Sister Teresa's acquaintance a few minutes later, that she had agreed to exchange duties. Sister Teresa was a delightful person, and Margaret fell under the spell of her gentle charm instantly, loving the small, wrinkled face beneath the spotless white coif the moment she set eyes on it.

She was a tiny little woman, of obviously frail physique, but the briskness of her movements and the competence with which she worked made her seem years younger than she was, and Margaret, guessing her age, put it at under sixty—to be utterly dumbfounded when the Sister herself confessed, smiling, to having recently passed her seventy-first birthday. Her blue eyes danced with good humour, her ready, eager smile was ageless, her gaiety infectious. Dr García had not exaggerated when he had said that she was a wonderful nurse. Her handling of Felipe was kindly and compassionate, yet she also made him laugh, and the boy took to her as quickly and wholeheartedly as he had taken to Margaret herself, so that she no longer worried about leaving him and he ceased to reproach her when she did.

Within half an hour of her arrival, Sister Teresa insisted that she could do everything that was necessary for their patient alone. As soon as they had gone through the casenotes together, she packed Margaret off to her room for the sleep she so badly needed. When, rested and refreshed, the British girl returned to the sickroom later in the afternoon to see if there were anything she could do, it was to be refused admittance with smiling but adamant firmness.

'If you have slept enough, child, then go out into the fresh air,' the old nun advised. 'We do not need you, Felipe and I, and I feel sure that, if you ask her, the Señora de Fontera will provide you with a car and a driver, so that you may see something of this beautiful country while you are here. Or, if today you do not feel energetic, go and sit in the *patio* by the fountain and relax. There is nothing for you to occupy yourself with here.'

Margaret, reluctant to approach the Marquesa with any sort of request on her own behalf, took the second part of this sage advice and went out to the *patio* with a book. It was deserted and delightfully cool and she seated herself on the parapet of the fountain, the book open on her knee, listening entranced to the musical sound of the falling water and feeling happier and more relaxed than she had done for days.

Her peace was, however, short-lived. First Pilar saw

her and, evidently acting on standing orders from their mistress, she and the major-domo carried out a table, chairs and the inevitable tray of tea, which they set ready for her, with many exclamations of pleasure because, at last, she was resting.

They were followed, shortly afterwards, by Carlos de Fontera, who came strolling slowly from the house to join her.

'Good evening, *señorita*,' he greeted, dark eyes meeting hers in mocking challenge. 'Is it permitted that I sit here and talk to you for a few minutes?'

'Of course, Don Carlos.' Margaret waved a hand in the direction of her tray. 'Perhaps you would like some tea?'

He shuddered faintly. 'Thank you, no.' He was smiling at her derisively. 'Tell me . . .' his voice held mockery too, 'is your stern guardian likely to come storming out to interrupt our *tête-à-tête*?'

'I don't think so,' Margaret assured him, colouring a little. 'Why should he?'

He spread his slim brown hands in a gesture of elaborate unconcern. 'He came yesterday and spoilt my plans, did he not? And then he dragged you away from a most delightful party. The de Gaulas are entertaining people, Miss Hay. You would have enjoyed their company had you stayed, I am sure.'

Margaret did not answer him. Remembering the condition in which she had found Felipe on her return, she was thankful that Julian *had* dragged her away, but it would scarcely be tactful to remind Carlos of this. He had meant well, he had been doing his best to amuse and entertain her, and . . . perhaps he didn't know about Felipe. She wondered whether the Marquesa had told him, but decided not to ask. The relationship between Carlos and his brother's widow still puzzled her a little; yesterday, she had sensed a certain hostility between them, but that might have been her own imagination. She could only suppose that, since they lived under the same roof, they must get on reasonably well together. The chauffeur, Ramón, had told her that Don Carlos administered the estate. He did this, presumably, on Felipe's behalf, until the boy should come of age, but no doubt he had money of his own and wasn't paid a salary, so that if he stayed, he must do so because it was what he wanted to do. Or perhaps he stayed for his mother's sake. She had formed the impression, she wasn't sure quite why, that Carlos was very devoted to old Doña Leandra.

'*Señorita* . . .' She looked up, startled, to find his gaze fixed on her face. He was no longer smiling and the expression in his dark eyes was grave.

'Yes?' she acknowledged.

'Tell me about last night,' he demanded, and when she hesitated, burst our irritably, 'Oh, you do not have to worry about giving away any secrets! I am aware of the bare facts. I have heard nothing else but reproaches from Louise all day because I took you and Julian away from here last night and did not return myself until the small hours. But how was I to know that anything untoward was likely to happen to the boy? It did not occur to me that a trained nurse would be so careless as to give the wrong drug to a patient under her care. I thought all drugs were clearly marked and that, in any case, they were kept safely under lock and key?'

'Yes,' Margaret agreed unhappily, 'they are clearly marked and we keep them locked up.'

'But in *this* case, despite such precautions, a mistake was made, was it not?'

'Apparently it was, Don Carlos. But—'

'By whom was the mistake made, Sister Hay?' he interrupted roughly. 'By Nurse Riardos?'

'I . . . don't know. Honestly, Don Carlos, that is the truth. I can't possibly tell you who made the mistake. There is no positive proof—'

'But it was a serious one?' Carlos persisted. 'The boy could have died, if you had stayed on with me at the

Ibañez, instead of coming back when you did?'

'I shouldn't like to say that,' Margaret evaded. 'I'm not a doctor. You should ask Mr Freyton.'

'Doctors, nurses—you are all the same!' Carlos complained, with bitterness. 'You will never commit yourselves. You must have positive proof, you say. And when a dangerous error is made, you will not admit to a layman how dangerous it was.'

'I'm sorry you think that,' Margaret told him. Her hand, she observed, was shaking. 'Don Carlos, I'm not trying to be deliberately obstructive, but Mr Freyton is the proper person for you to ask about this matter, not me. As a nurse, my responsibility is limited to carrying out his orders and to caring for the patient to the best of my ability, but—'

Again he interrupted her, his voice low and angry. 'Were you not responsible for the safe custody of the drugs, Sister Hay? Did you not have the key in your possession?'

'I was responsible for the drugs, Don Carlos. But I don't keep the key to them when I am off duty.'

His expression softened. 'No, of course you do not. Sister Hay, do not misunderstand me—I am not blaming *you* for what happened. By running away from my party, which upset me a good deal at the time, you saved Felipe's life, I imagine. No'—as she attempted to deny it—'please do not try to tell me that you did not, when I know better.' He put out a hand to grasp hers and Margaret saw that, like her own, it was trembling. 'I have the greatest and most sincere admiration for you— as a nurse and as a woman. Please believe that.'

She coloured. 'Thank you, Don Carlos. It's kind of you to say so.'

But he wasn't listening. 'You do not know the situation here,' he said, and Margaret was reminded of Julian's words to her in the taxi. Julian had told her that she did not understand the situation and then he had said, bitterly, that she did not know Carlos. Or something to that effect. It was true, of course, she knew nothing of either, but she was coming to know Carlos and she felt, suddenly, acutely sorry for him. He was evidently very fond of little Felipe and upset at the thought of what had happened to him. And yesterday, before the operation, he had come to the boy's room to pray for him . . .

'Sister Hay,' Carlos said gravely, 'Everything here—' He waved a hand about him, the gesture taking in the vast, palatial house at their back, with its rows of windows, and the extensive grounds of the estate, which they could not see. 'Everything belongs to Felipe—he was my brother's only son and his heir. The name is his, the title, the estate, the de Fontera fortune which, even by today's standards, is considerable. And I have nothing, you understand—or by comparison, it is nothing. But if Felipe were to die . . .' His pause was studied and significant. 'If Felipe were to die, Sister Hay, all this would be mine.'

Margaret stared at him, bewildered and at a loss for words. She managed at last, through stiff lips, to confess wretchedly that she did not understand what he was trying to tell her.

'You do not? But it is simple.' Carlos got to his feet, a tall, slim, attractive stranger, whose smile lacked any pretence of amusement now. He said, looking down at her, 'If Nurse Riardos made a mistake with that morphine, then—although unfortunate—it was just a mistake, was it not? And Felipe suffered no serious harm. I have been to visit him, with his new nurse, and I have seen that he is happy, without a care and getting well and gaining strength, which is exactly as it should be. But, Sister Hay . . .' Again he paused, his mouth compressed.

'Yes?' Margaret prompted apprehensively, her heart suddenly beating very fast.

'If Nurse Riardos did *not* make a mistake,' Carlos stated carefully, 'then the drug must have been given, not by accident but deliberately. Whoever gave it may try again, don't you think? And I do not want to inherit Felipe's fortune, *señorita*, because someone has taken his life. That is the last thing I want, believe me.'

Margaret was impressed by his evident sincerity. But his deductions, following the line of her own reasoning, brought all her doubts and fears flooding back into her mind. She touched his arm. 'How will you find out?' she asked. 'Will you go and see Nurse Riardos?'

He shrugged. 'Sister, I have spent most of today searching for her, without success.'

'But Ramón drove her back to Barcelona last night, didn't he? I thought—'

'Yes.' Carlos put in, his eyes very bright, 'that is so. Ramón drove her back to the rooms where she lodges, when she is not working. But I was told when I called there that she had gone out, early this morning, without leaving word as to her whereabouts. Since then I have been back there twice, the last time about an hour ago.' He spread his hands helplessly. 'She was not there.'

This was a totally unexpected complication, and for a moment, Margaret was taken aback by it. Then, recalling her plea to Julian, she said earnestly, 'Don Carlos, would it not be safer to move Felipe to a nursing home or hospital in Barcelona? Surely there, with a large, trained staff to watch over him, he would be in less danger? Couldn't you persuade your sister-in-law to let us move him?'

Carlos considered this suggestion, brows knit in a thoughtful frown. 'I do not think that Louise would hear of it . . . unless your Mr Freyton added his persuasions to mine. She might listen to him, perhaps, although I know that *she* feels Felipe is safer here than anywhere else. That was why she went to so much trouble to arrange for the operation to be performed here, in this house . . . she never lets the boy out of her sight, you know. Certainly she has never done so in the past, she has always kept him with her, for fear that something should happen to him. I remember once before that—' He broke off abruptly, but Margaret, sensing what he had been about to tell her, asked quickly, 'Don Carlos, has anything—anything like this—ever happened before?'

'What do you mean?'

'I mean has there been anything, anything at all in the past that might have led you to believe that Felipe's life was in danger?'

He expelled his breath in a longdrawn sigh. 'There have been accidents,' he admitted, and then shook his head. 'No, I cannot honestly tell you that these led me to believe that a deliberate threat against Felipe was ever intended. Some children are accident-prone—isn't that the correct term for it? Felipe is—he has been, ever since he was a baby, and as he was a cripple it was harder for him to avoid them. He has a weak body, poor child, coupled with an adventurous spirit. Once he nearly drowned, when he was fishing in the trout stream by the entrance lodge, but fortunately his grandmother, Doña Leandra, was nearby and she heard his screams. On another occasion, he fell from a tree and broke his arm . . . oh, there have been quite a succession of such accidents, but all of them the kind that might befall any small boy. The most serious was about a year ago, when he mistook a box of Doña Leandra's sleeping tablets for sweets and consumed about half the box.'

'What happened?' Margaret pursued, when he stopped.

'Oh, Dr García was promptly on the scene. We had some very anxious hours, but the good doctor pulled him through.'

There seemed, on the face of it, nothing more to be gained by discussing the accidents, Margaret decided. They were, as Carlos had said, the kind that any adventurous boy might stumble into, especially if, like Felipe, he were crippled. Some children were undoubtedly more accident-prone than others. And although it seemed strange that a boy of—what, nearly eleven?—should have mistaken sleeping tablets for sweets, no doubt Doña Leandra, being old and perhaps not as observant as she might have been, had left them within his reach.

She glanced quickly at Carlos. 'Mr Freyton promised that he would ask the Marquesa about having Felipe moved,' she confided.

'And you'd like me to ask her too?'

'Yes, I would. I'd feel happier if she would agree to our doing so.'

'Even with Sister Teresa to help you guard him?' he questioned, smiling.

Margaret found herself echoing his smile. 'I am much happier now that *she* is here, Don Carlos, I must admit.'

'I do not hold out much hope of success, either for Julian Freyton or myself,' Carlos told her, 'but, since you wish it, I will speak to Louise.'

'Thank you,' Margaret answered, with relief. She wanted to tell him about her nightmare experience in Felipe's sickroom, if only in order to convince him of the urgency of her request, but, aware that she had no proof, she hesitated. She had told Julian and he hadn't believed her; was Carlos, in spite of all he had just said, any more likely to take her seriously? He might be but . . . they had no proof of anything, until one of them could see and speak to Nurse Riardos. And none of it would matter, if only Felipe's mother would agree to his being moved.

'I hope,' she said, 'that you will manage to persuade the Marquesa, Don Carlos.'

'I shall do my best,' he assured her, 'although'—he was frowning again—'suppose, for the purpose of argument, Sister Hay, there *is* someone who intends harm to Felipe, do you imagine that the fact that he is taken for a few weeks to a nursing home would end the danger to him? He will have to come back here eventually, will he not, to face the same danger? If it exists at all, it comes from inside, from one of those living in this house. It comes from someone who, for some reason, would like to see me in Felipe's place.'

Margaret felt the colour drain slowly from her cheeks. Did he, she wondered, know who the someone was—did he suspect? It seemed that he must, for his next words were uttered with barely controlled anger. 'I should like to put an end to it, if it exists, *señorita*, once and for all. I should like to *know* if it does exist, to find out who is responsible. And my best chance of finding out will be when you and Sister Teresa are with Felipe constantly and always on the alert, here—in this house, not shut away in some nursing home in the city. I think it would be better and, in the long run, safer for Felipe if he stays here, do you know that?'

She followed his reasoning, but it frightened her. She wanted to protest, but the words wouldn't come, and he said, the anger fading from his voice, 'Bear with me, will you not? At least until I have contacted Nurse Riardos and confirmed what I am convinced is the truth. You are convinced of it too, I am sure, Sister Hay. You know that Riardos would not have made so terrible a mistake, don't you?'

She did, Margaret recognised, but she was silent.

Carlos put out a hand and, very gently and diffidently, recaptured hers and bore it to his lips. 'You are a brave girl,' he told her softly, 'and you are fond of Felipe, as I am. No one could help it, I think . . . save this one person, who regards his possessions as of more importance than he is. Yet this person loves me, that is what makes it so very complex and difficult, you understand. I dare not accuse, without proof, but I do not want the proof to be the little Felipe's death, *señorita*.'

'No,' Margaret said, her voice a whisper. She, too, had begun to have suspicions now, but she could not voice them. As Carlos had said, there had to be proof. She asked, speaking her thoughts aloud and unaware that she had asked the question until the words were out,

'Don Carlos, when you came back last night, did you come into the sickroom? Did you lock the door from the outside and push the key under it, for me to find when I . . . when I woke up?'

His eyes narrowed. 'No, Sister Hay, I did not.' He waited, eyeing her curiously, and when she did not speak, said tonelessly, 'So you, too, slept on duty, did you? Have you, perhaps, some explanation to give me?'

Margaret sighed. 'I have one, but I don't even know that it's the truth, I'm afraid.' She told him and saw the thick, dark brows crease into a frown again.

'You say María brought you coffee, on Louise's orders?'

'Yes. I was glad of it. I was tired, you see, and I hoped it would keep me awake. But'—she looked up at him miserably—'it didn't, it did just the reverse, or it seemed to . . . and in the morning, the tray had gone.'

He was silent for a long moment, thinking hard. Then he said, 'Of course, you were tired . . . you must have been exhausted. It's possible that you slept naturally, but only possible; and there remains another possibility, which we've got to face. But it was inhuman to expect you to sit up all night with Felipe, after being on duty all day. And you were up at dawn, weren't you? What was Julian thinking of to allow it? Did he not offer to relieve you or suggest that one of the servants should do so— Pilar or María? María was Felipe's nurse, when he was a baby—she is absolutely devoted to him.'

'Julian Freyton arranged to relieve me after the first two hours,' Margaret admitted reluctantly. 'But—'

'But he, too, slept?' Carlos put in. 'Is that what you are trying to tell me?'

'Yes.'

'I see.' His voice was still flat and expressionless, devoid of emotion as he added, 'This, I think, confirms my suspicions . . . don't you agree?'

'I . . . I'm afraid it must,' Margaret conceded. He leaned towards her, an odd glint in his dark eyes. 'Sister

Hay, we have got to find out the truth—now, in the next few weeks, while Felipe is in your care. May I count on your help?'

Margaret hesitated for a long time before giving her agreement. She was conscious of many misgivings and she asked, in a small, unhappy voice, if Carlos intended to confide in Julian Freyton. 'I must, if you don't. After all, he is the surgeon who operated on Felipe, he is in charge of the case. And if he has succeeded in persuading the Marquesa to allow the boy to be moved, then I should have to back him up, since it was my suggestion in the first place and I asked him to speak to her.'

'That is understood,' Carlos assured her briefly. 'And I shall tell Julian all that I have told you, *señorita* . . . if he will listen to me.'

'He will listen. Why shouldn't he?'

Carlos shrugged. 'At one time,' he returned, with harsh emphasis, 'Julian Freyton was engaged to be married to Louise. Perhaps you did not know that? It was, of course, before she met my brother, when she—like yourself, Sister Hay—was training to become a nurse.'

'The Marquesa . . . is a nurse?' Margaret stared at him, unable to believe the evidence of her own ears. A flood of contradictory suspicions, confused memories and fresh doubts came surging into her mind. She remembered Louise de Fontera's arrogance, her refusal to admit her to social equality or even to eat with her, and then, most damning of all, she remembered last night. Louise de Fontera had summarily dismissed Nurse Riardos, but, although a trained nurse herself, she hadn't taken Riardos' place in the sickroom at her son's bedside—she had delegated the task to poor, frail old Doña Leandra. And when she had come, later on, to visit the boy, she hadn't offered to relieve Margaret herself, who had been on duty throughout the long, exhausting day; she had simply come in, with her usual cold hauteur, and left again after only a few minutes. She . . .

But Carlos was explaining, and she forced herself to concentrate on what he was telling her. Julian, it appeared, had gone as a young, newly qualified surgeon, to work in the American hospital where Louise was training. They had become engaged, she had followed him back to Europe when her training was completed, coming over as nurse to an ailing South American millionaire, whom she had accompanied to Barcelona, where—a few months afterwards—she had met José de Fontera.

'My brother was an infinitely better *parti* than Julian,' Carlos said, with cynical bitterness. His hands described an angry little gesture in the air. 'He was already ill and Louise nursed him. She went with him on a cruise, which he took in the faint hope of restoring his health, and they were married as soon as the cruise ended and the ship returned to Barcelona. Naturally, my family were opposed to the match, but none of us could prevent it . . . José was dying, it was his last wish, and so it was granted. He died three months before Felipe was born, of leukaemia, Sister Hay. And Julian—' He broke off abruptly.

'And . . . Julian?' Margaret questioned. She sensed that there must be more and wondered if he would tell her, but he answered, tight-lipped, 'Julian was heart-broken. And so were we, when Felipe was born a cripple. But although his birth deprived me of my inheritance, I do not want him to die, *señorita*, and I begrudge him nothing that is rightly his. Remember this, I beg you.'

He turned then and left her, walking with swift, impatient strides back to the house. Margaret stood watching his tall, lean figure until it was out of sight, a prey to the most conflicting fears and emotions that she had ever experienced in her life.

She was no nearer the solution of any of the problems that faced her when, after the evening meal had been served to her in her room, she went to relieve

Sister Teresa for the night.

But Felipe, at least, was so much improved and in such high spirits, despite the heavy plaster cast which enveloped his small, pain-twisted body, that she forgot her own disquiet and laughed with him, as she prepared to settle him for the night.

He was brimming over with mischief, splashing her gleefully with the water she had brought to the bedside for his evening sponge and giggling like any small, naughty boy as he surveyed the ruin of her once impeccably starched apron-front.

'Oh, Sister Margarita, this is such fun!' he told her, seizing her hands in his warm, soapy ones, and then, like a puppy which had suddenly tired after a strenuous game, his thin little face relaxed and he was asleep almost before Margaret had finished his toilet.

She stood looking down at him, feeling the tears come to ache in her throat as she studied the bony contours of his face and saw the familiar smile which, it seemed, always lit it when he slept. He was so young, so helpless and vulnerable, so endearing. She wanted impulsively to put her arms round him and hold him close, to give him some, at least, of the love and affection he lacked and which his mother, all too evidently, did not feel for him. But instead the habit of years made her set to work straightening up the bed, tidying the room and putting away the washing things she had been using, and the little boy slept on, oblivious.

Julian Freyton came in, just as she had finished her self-imposed task. Margaret pulled down her sleeves and reached for her cuffs, but he shook his head and called her over to the window, where their voices would not disturb the sleeping child.

'I examined him earlier this evening,' he said, 'when Sister Teresa was on duty. I came to see you, Margaret.'

'Yes?' Margaret answered, and waited.

He sighed. 'How are you and Sister Teresa getting on?'

It wasn't the question she had expected, but she replied to it readily. 'Very well indeed. She is everything Dr García said she was, and Felipe adores her.'

'I'm glad of that because . . . Margaret, I've talked to Louise de Fontera, as you asked me to, about having Felipe moved, and I'm afraid she won't hear of it. She insists that he must remain here.'

'Insists?' Margaret echoed.

'Yes, I'm afraid so. In fact, she's quite adamant about it—even to the extent of dispensing with *your* services, if necessary.'

'And taking my place, Mr Freyton?' Margaret suggested, unable to keep the note of resentment from sounding in her voice. 'Because she could, couldn't she? I mean, she is a trained nurse, I believe.'

Julian Freyton was silent for a long time. His face, Margaret saw, was strained and unhappy, his mouth a hard, taut line, and a small pulse, which was always there when he was agitated or upset, was beating furiously at the angle of his jaw.

'You too, Margaret?' he said at last, with more sadness than anger.

'I . . . don't know what you're implying, I—'

'I think you do,' he returned wearily. 'You've been talking to Carlos, haven't you? Well, he has also talked to me. I know what he thinks and what he's afraid of, he's made no secret of it. But it isn't true, Margaret. I give you my solemn word that it isn't.'

'You mean that his suspicions aren't true? That Felipe isn't in danger or—'

'No, no,' Julian Freyton broke in painfully, 'not that. The poor child may be in danger, though I hope to heaven he's not.' He took her by the shoulders, forcing her to look at him. 'If he is, then it is largely Carlos' doing. Margaret'—his fingers bit into her shoulders— 'Carlos believes that Felipe is my son.'

Margaret stood transfixed, her eyes wide with shocked astonishment. 'But he'—even to her own ears, her voice sounded unnaturally high-pitched—'he *isn't*, is he? He couldn't be . . .'

'Of course he's not!' Julian's repudiation of the suggestion was explosive and fraught with bitterness, but it was wholly convincing, and she knew a swift and heady relief as she recognised its truth. 'Then why—' she began, only to be cut short.

'Don't you see?' Julian flung at her, his face white. 'Carlos may have talked to others about this. Apparently he's thought it for some time, although he has only just seen fit to tell me so. Margaret, if Felipe is in danger, it's because someone else in this house shares Carlos' belief. That can be the only reason.'

'But it's not the Marquesa,' Margaret whispered, 'because she *knows* it isn't true.'

He nodded slowly, with certainty.

'Then who?' she asked miserably, '*who?*'

'I don't know, Margaret. I wish to God I did. In this house, it might be anyone.'

They stood there, looking at each other, and the silence of the vast house closed about them, became a tangible thing, pregnant with menace. At last Julian said heavily, 'We've got to find out who it is or the boy will never be safe. I've moved my room. I'll be next door, within call, if you need me during the night . . . and *I'll* test your coffee, before you drink it. Goodnight, Margaret. Call out at once, if you want me—don't hesitate.'

'I won't,' she promised. She walked with him to the door. The key was in the lock, on the inside, and they both looked at it.

'Lock it, if you'd prefer to,' he invited, 'but my door will be open.'

Margaret shook her head, suddenly resolute. 'No,' she said, 'I won't lock it, Julian.'

He bent swiftly and she felt his lips brush her cheek. Then he had gone and the shadowed room was silent again.

CHAPTER TEN

THE night, which she had feared so much, passed swiftly and uneventfully for Margaret and her small, helpless patient.

After a brief visit from Louise de Fontera, who said little and seemed scarcely to spare a glance for her son, no one else came near the sickroom, until Pilar brought coffee and sandwiches just before midnight. A note, in Julian's handwriting, lay on the tray, propped up against the flask. It said, briefly, that he had suffered no ill-effects from drinking it and, thus reassured, Margaret helped herself from the flask gratefully.

At midnight, Julian looked in, to make a formal inspection of Felipe's chart; he came again, in dressing gown and pyjamas, at three, and, at seven, shared Margaret's early morning tea.

'No misadventures?' he asked her, smiling.

'None,' Margaret told him, 'thank goodness.'

He glanced across to the bed and shivered in the cool morning air. 'Perhaps there won't be any more,' he said, but in her heart Margaret was aware that neither of them believed it. Julian passed her his cup. 'I'd like another, if you've some to spare . . . I'm finding it hard to wake up.'

'You didn't get much sleep?' she suggested, picking up the teapot.

'More than you did, I expect. I'm still feeling guilty about the night before, Margaret. And I'm worried about you.'

'You needn't be.' She passed him his refilled cup, her hand quite steady. 'Now that I know, it's . . . well, not less frightening or horrible, of course, but easier to endure. I was caught completely unprepared the other night. I mean, it never occurred to me that my coffee might have been drugged, and so I didn't take any steps to safeguard Felipe before I passed out. But now I *am* prepared."

He eyed her searchingly over the rim of his teacup.

'You're still convinced that your coffee was drugged?'

'Yes, I am.' Margaret faced him, meeting his gaze directly. 'I'm not in the habit of going to sleep on duty, however tired I may be. In all the years of my training, even when I was a pro doing my first night duty, I never fell asleep.'

'I believe you.' Julian set down his cup. 'Who,' he asked, 'do you think came in and removed the remains of your drugged coffee?'

Margaret sighed. 'I've racked my brains, but I honestly haven't an idea. Unless it was María. She's the only one who knew I'd had it, because she brought it to me.'

'And do you suppose *she* locked the door?'

'If it was María who came in, then I think she might have done that. She was Felipe's nannie and she worships him, there's simply no doubt of it. I haven't talked to her much, because she doesn't speak more than a few words of English, but I think she's intelligent and, as I say, devoted to Felipe. *She* would have been capable of locking the door, to make certain that he was safe.'

Julian got up and walked over to the window. He said, over his shoulder, 'But that suggests that María was aware that Felipe was in danger, doesn't it?'

'I suppose it does,' Margaret conceded.

'And, carrying the supposition a little further, if she was aware that the danger existed, she must also know from whom it came?'

'Y . . . yes. If it *was* María who locked the door.'

'We're up against a blank wall again, aren't we?' Julian spoke irritably. 'But I'll try and have a talk with María today, if I can. She certainly seems the most likely person to have come in and, as you mentioned, she was the only one who knew you'd had the coffee.'

'Except . . .' Margaret began, and bit off the words. He turned from his contemplation of the scene outside the window.

'Except Louise, who apparently ordered it for you?' he offered. 'Was that what you were going to say?'

Margaret felt the hot, embarrassed colour rise to burn in her cheeks. 'I didn't say it,' she pointed out. He left the window and came to stand beside her, frowning. She rose.

'It . . . it's time I woke Felipe. Sister Teresa will be here soon and I want to leave everything ready for her. So if you don't mind, Julian, I—'

'I do mind, Sister Margarita.' He didn't smile as he used Felipe's nickname for her. 'Spare me just a minute or two more, won't you?'

'Yes, of course. If you want me to.'

'I want to get one or two things absolutely clear, Margaret,' he said brusquely. 'First, you need not imagine that you are sparing *my* feelings when you refrain from mentioning Louise de Fontera's name in connection with what we have just been talking about. As I told you and as I believe you also learnt from Carlos, I met Louise in America fourteen years ago, when we were both working in New York. I was twenty-three at the time and I'd just qualified; I was an idealistic young fool, with my head right up in the clouds, and I put every woman I met on a pedestal. Louise was very lovely, and the pedestal I set her on would have dwarfed Nelson's column.' He smiled wryly. 'I asked her to marry me when I'd known her for a couple of weeks, believe it or not!'

Margaret said nothing. She studiously avoided his gaze, but, for some reason, her heart had quickened its beat.

'Well, you know the rest of the story, because Carlos told you, didn't he? Louise left the States a month or so after I did and she worked her passage to Europe by acting as nurse to a Uruguayan millionaire, who wanted to die in his native Spain. She met José de Fontera and accompanied him on a Mediterranean cruise before I saw her again . . . and when I did see her, it was to be told, rather firmly and brutally, that she intended to marry him. I was cut up, my illusions were shattered and—like the idiot I was—I moved heaven and earth to try and get her to change her mind, but she wouldn't listen to me. When I met José, I didn't try any more . . . I liked him immensely and we became—surprisingly—the best of friends. I even acted as best man at his wedding.'

'Did you?' Margaret said softly.

He sighed. 'Poor devil, he was suffering from leukaemia and there was nothing anyone could do for him, but what there was, I did. I made him come to London, with Louise, to see one of the men I was then working under at Bart's, and he tried everything . . . but without success. We had to fall back on blood transfusions and we kept him alive with those. He came back here, with Louise, and died three months before Felipe was born.' Again his gaze went, as if drawn there against his will, to the bed. 'I was idiot enough to be pleased that Louise had had a son, Margaret.'

She felt his pain and was silent. Julian squared his shoulders. 'I'm telling you this so that you'll understand how utterly impossible Carlos' suggestion is,' he said bitterly. After a pause, he went on, his voice devoid of feeling, 'I did not see Louise de Fontera again until she brought Felipe to me in Harley Street eight months ago. I wanted to operate then, but she wouldn't hear of it. When, after taking him to umpteen other physicians and surgeons, she finally made the decision to allow it and asked me to perform the operation here, I couldn't refuse, Margaret, because I knew how much it meant to her to have his deformity cured. And besides . . .' He hesitated. 'I don't know if you'll understand this, but the reason why she . . . why she can't regard him with the normal affection a mother feels for her child is because he *is* deformed. She told me that a long time ago, in a letter. And she repeated it again, the evening we arrived here . . . she broke down completely and wept in my arms.' He shook his head, as if to rid himself of a hurtful memory, which still lingered, in spite of his anxiety to forget it.

Watching him, Margaret felt her throat tighten. She asked, hardly recognising her own voice, 'Were you in the balcony room, the one that looks out on to the fountain in the *patio*?'

Julian turned to glance at her quickly, his eyes narrowed.

'Yes,' he admitted, 'we were. And was it you who came in, Margaret?' When she nodded, wordlessly, he expelled his breath in a long and heartfelt sigh. 'I can imagine what you thought!'

'Can you?' she challenged bitterly.

'Yes . . . especially since I'd told you that it was all over years ago. And it was, Margaret. I can only ask you to believe that . . . and to believe that there are some things a man does out of pity, rather than passion. There are some situations which . . .' He looked at her, with a sudden boyish helplessness. 'I don't know how to make you understand,' he said at last, humbly. 'I can only hope that you do.'

'I'm trying to, Julian. But I don't think I do. I—I wish I could. It upsets me, to see you, to think that you . . . oh, I don't know.'

'Another who puts people on pedestals?' he suggested wryly.

'Yes, I—suppose so.'

His hand came out, very gently, to touch her cheek.

'If you only knew the truth, Margaret! But there it is . . .' He withdrew his hand, smiling at her uncertainly. '*Don't* you know it?'

'No,' she confessed, not looking at him but more aware of him, standing there beside her, than she had ever been of any man before. Even the light and gentle touch of his fingers hurt her unbearably and she dared not meet his gaze.

'Then I shall have to prove it to you, shan't I? Beyond all shadow of doubt . . .' His voice was very quiet and he made no move to touch her again. 'This afternoon, Margaret'—his tone altered, became brisk—'I'm going to borrow a car and go to one of the beaches. I should like you to come with me. Will you, please?'

Across the room, a faint sound drew Margaret's attention to the bed. Felipe was stirring, it was nearly eight o'clock, and at eight, her mind registered, Sister Teresa would be here. As always, the habit of discipline and training proved too strong to resist. She smoothed her apron and automatically felt for the watch pinned to her bib.

'Felipe is awake. I must go to him, Julian.'

His smile widened. 'Being you, obviously you must, Sister Hay . . . and I won't detain you. I don't want Sister Teresa to come in and catch me in this somewhat unprofessional attire. But I'd so much like it if you would come with me this afternoon. Please say that you will, because that will mean that at least you trust me to tell you the truth.'

'Thank you,' Margaret said, intending to make her acceptance formal, but, looking up into his face, the expression she saw in it sent the unruly colour rushing to her cheeks. 'I'd love to come,' she told him truthfully, and her heart, against all reason, was singing as she went to rouse Felipe.

Dr García came, before Margaret went off duty. He was delighted at the patient's progress and congratulated her heartily on the way in which she had won Sister Teresa's approval.

'The good Sister is not easy to please,' he confided, smiling from one to the other of them but reserving his warmest smile for the old nun. 'I am sure that our young Marqués is in the best of hands now, and that we need have no more fears for his well-being.'

Fervently, Margaret echoed his hope as she left him to examine Felipe with Sister Teresa, and went in search of breakfast.

She slept until almost four o'clock, when Pilar called her with tea and the news, delivered with tears in her eyes, and many hysterical sobs, that Doña Leandra had been taken ill quite unexpectedly.

'She suffers from her heart, *señorita*, you understand. Not severely until now, and Dr García gives her tablets to take which almost always are enough to make her well again. But this time . . . ah, it is a tragedy! This time, she is stricken so that she cannot speak, and both Dr García and the English doctor who came with you to cure the little Don Felipe . . . both had to go to her, *señorita*, and they were with her all morning while you were sleeping.'

'You should have wakened me,' Margaret reproached her, instantly concerned. 'Perhaps I could have helped them.'

'The English doctor said that you were not to be disturbed, *señorita*,' Pilar protested. 'Sister Teresa helped them and María and I sat with Don Felipe, until she had finished. Now yet another nurse has come, from the convent, and it is she who now cares for Doña Leandra.'

Margaret dressed hurriedly, but when she reported to the sickroom, Sister Teresa assured her calmly that everything that could be done had been done and that Doña Leandra was so much better that she would probably not need a night nurse.

'The women servants will attend to her, and María has experience of her attacks. If you are able, perhaps, to look at her once or twice during the night, that will be all she will require, and in the meantime there is nothing for you to do but enjoy your few remaining hours of freedom. I understand from Mr Freyton that he is taking you for a drive to Castello Delmonte? Go, then, and enjoy yourself! Doña Leandra has an anginal condition, but she is not seriously ill, and our little Felipe, as you can see, is in the best of health.' She waved a hand in Felipe's direction and he grinned back delightedly.

'Castello Delmonte is a wonderful place, Sister Margarita,' he told her, and went into ecstatic details of the last visit he had paid to the beach. 'Next time I go there, I shall be able to learn to swim properly, shall I not? Just like you and Mr Freyton.'

'Of course you will, child,' Sister Teresa promised. She added, to Margaret's amusement, 'And *you* will need a hat and a parasol, Sister Hay, if you are not to suffer sunburn and spoil your lovely English-rose complexion!'

Margaret dutifully fetched a hat from her room. On her way downstairs, she met Louise de Fontera, who looked with raised eyebrows at her linen dress and beach bag and said coldly, 'I understood that you were sleeping.'

'I was,' Margaret answered, forcing herself to smile.

'And now?' the Marquesa demanded.

'I am going out—to Castello Delmonte, with Mr Freyton.' She added a few words of sympathy for Doña Leandra, but Louise de Fontera silenced her with a swift, imperious gesture.

'Doña Leandra is recovering, I believe. She is old, she has angina . . . these things happen, I guess. Hers is not a tragedy like my son's, is it?'

'No—no, of course not.' Margaret was puzzled by her attitude. If not callous, it was certainly very close to indifference. But the Marquesa's next words surprised her still more. 'Sister Hay'—the slender, beautiful hand rested for a moment on her bare arm, its fine solitaire diamond glinting in the light from a window above their heads—'tell me honestly, please—*is* the operation on Felipe successful? Will he be completely cured?'

'You should know,' Margaret told her deliberately, 'as a trained nurse, Señora de Fontera, that I can't possibly answer that question. Mr Freyton is the surgeon who performed the operation and he is the proper person to ask.'

The Marquesa caught her breath on a sigh. 'I have asked him, several times. He says it was successful.'

'Then why aren't you satisfied? Don't you believe him?'

'Yes, I guess so. But he knows what it means to me. I don't think he'd tell me if it weren't. I think you would, though—in fact, I'm sure you would.'

'Why are you sure I would?' Margaret challenged.

Louise de Fontera smiled faintly. It was, Margaret thought, the first time her patient's mother had given her a smile that could be considered genuine. 'Why?' she repeated. 'Oh, that's easy, Miss Hay—because you dislike me so intensely. You do, don't you?'

'If I'm to be honest . . . you've scarcely given me the chance to do anything else, have you?'

'Perhaps not. But carry on being honest, please. *Why* do you dislike me?'

'Chiefly because of the way you behave to Felipe. You come to see him, but you don't speak to him—I've never seen you kiss him. He needs so much that only you can give him—affection, trust, your love . . . ' Now that she had been invited to speak freely, Margaret talked on, warming to her subject, and the Marquesa, a little to her surprise, heard her out in silence, making no attempt to defend herself. 'Even if the operation is a hundred per cent successful—as I believe it will be,' she ended, 'that won't be enough. Felipe has a mind, as well as a body, you know. You can't cure the one if you neglect the other.'

'Have you quite done?' the Marquesa asked, without anger, her voice level.

'Yes, I've done. I'm sorry if I've offended you, but you asked me to be honest and I was. I told you exactly what I think.'

'You haven't offended me in the least. But you

haven't been entirely honest, have you? You have another, much stronger reason for disliking me, Miss Hay.'

Margaret reddened. 'Have I, madame?'

'Oh, don't be so formal . . . my name is Louise. Since we're both members of the same profession, we might as well drop the ceremony, don't you think?'

'Certainly, if you wish. My name is Margaret.'

'I know.' Again the faint, derisive smile. 'I mustn't keep you from your outing with Julian, must I? Because I can see that you're longing to go, and I expect he's waiting for you with his usual impatience. But'—her smile faded and the blue eyes met Margaret's with all their accustomed hostility—'Julian is the real reason for your dislike of me, isn't he? You imagine he's still in love with me . . . perhaps you even believe this utterly fantastic story Carlos has told you? I can assure you that is completely untrue and I can also tell you, with absolute honesty, that Julian isn't in love with me. Or I with him.'

'I . . . see,' Margaret stammered, very much at a loss. 'Why are you telling me all this, Louise?'

Louise de Fontera shrugged her slim, elegant shoulders.

'I think I owe it to you to tell you. You've been good to Felipe—it's possible that you saved his life the other night. You may think that I don't care about Felipe, but that's not true either, because I care for him very much. Too much, perhaps . . . and one day, if you'll listen, I'll try to tell you why I've been unable to show him *how* much. It's a long and very involved story and I guess that only a psychiatrist would really understand it. But if you'd had to watch the man you loved more than anyone else in the world die slowly, inch by inch, while you stood by, powerless to do a thing to prevent it . . . well, I guess you might be something like I am now, Margaret Hay. And one thing I guarantee, you'd be scared stiff of it happening again.'

'You mean . . . to Felipe?' Margaret said, very gently now.

The proud golden head was bowed. 'I mean to Felipe,' Louise de Fontera answered bitterly. Then, with an abrupt change of mood, she waved Margaret in the direction of the door. 'Go on, go on!' she urged impatiently. 'You've only got till eight, haven't you? Then don't waste your time, for any sake. Go out and look for him. You'll find him in the garage, I imagine. And I hope to heaven that when *you* marry, you'll get a better deal than I had—though it's possible you deserve it more. And that you've got more courage than I have. Because I didn't even have enough to go on living!'

Feeling considerably shaken, Margaret left her. She found Julian at the wheel of a black limousine, smaller than the one which had met them at the airport but still a fairly large and luxuriously fitted vehicle. He said, holding open the door of the passenger's seat for her, 'I was just about to send a search party to look for you. We said four-thirty, didn't we?'

'Yes, we did.'

'What held you up?'

'Louise de Fontera did,' Margaret confessed wryly.

In the act of starting the engine, he turned to look at her in some astonishment. 'Were you talking to her?' he asked.

'Yes, I was. Very . . . freely, I suppose you'd call it. Julian, what a strange woman she is. I'm afraid I don't understand her, but just now I came nearer to understanding her than I ever have before. Or at least . . . to liking her.'

He swung the big car round deftly and drove out into the long, tree-lined avenue. They had almost reached the lodge before he spoke. Then he said flatly, 'I'm glad you found you could like her and glad that she talked to you, because I think it might help her. She has very few friends and is too much alone for a woman of her age.'

'Very few friends?' Margaret exclaimed incredulously. 'But surely with a title and money and this magnificent estate, she can't lack friends? I should have thought—'

Julian shook his head. 'Her title is just a name, Margaret. The de Fonteras disapproved of the marriage and of her, and they have never really accepted her. Oh, she has money, there's plenty of that, and admittedly she lives here and the servants wait on her and pay her lip-service, because she is Felipe's mother. But there it ends. The servants, in their superstitious, peasant's way, blame *her* for the fact that the boy is crippled, and their loyalty is to old Doña Leandra and to Carlos—to Jaime, when he's at home, and, of course, to Felipe.'

'So long as they have no doubt as to his parentage?' Margaret suggested, and he nodded grimly.

'Quite! Louise doesn't entertain here, as you've probably realised. The de Fonteras' friends despise her and her own kind of people aren't acceptable to old Doña Leandra, so—' He sighed. 'She is lonely and heartbroken—because, you see, she was deeply and sincerely in love with her husband.'

They reached the lodge and Julian pulled up, waiting for the lodge-keeper to come out and open the gates. When he had done so and they resumed their drive, he continued to talk about Louise de Fontera. Through the years, it seemed, Louise had written to him, clinging desperately to his friendship.

'I don't think,' he admitted, his tone rueful, 'that she ever really loved me. Ours was a boy-and-girl thing that wouldn't have lasted and certainly couldn't compare with what she felt for José . . . and he for her. None of the de Fonteras give her credit for that, you know—they won't recognise that theirs was a love match, and insist that Louise married for what she thought she could get out of José. I know that isn't so because I saw a great deal of them after they were first married, and José, as I told you, was one of my closest friends. He was an exceptionally fine fellow and his death was one of those senselessly cruel things that destroy one's faith in God.' His hands moved, tightening their grip on the steering wheel. 'I know it went a long way towards destroying mine.'

Margaret was silent, waiting. She sensed that he wanted to unburden himself and that it would help her to know him if she listened.

'I suppose,' he went on, 'that for the past ten years, anyway, I've been about the only real friend Louise has had. We didn't see each other, but we wrote—perhaps five or six times a year. No more than that, but it kept us in touch, and because she knew I wouldn't abuse her confidence, she told me more about her life here than I imagine she ever allowed anyone else to find out. She is a proud person, Margaret, and a very controlled one, and to the rest of the world in general—and to the de Fonteras in particular—she didn't betray her feelings, she hid them behind a mask and gave them back as good as she got. Better, perhaps, on occasions . . . especially when she attempted to have old Doña Leandra treated by a psychiatrist.'

'She did that?' Margaret turned to him, eyes wide with mingled pity and surprise.

'Unsuccessfully,' Julian returned. Brief anger flared in his eyes and then faded. 'Carlos and Jaime wouldn't hear of it, of course—the mere suggestion was taken as an affront. But the old lady is undeniably senile and extremely odd in her behaviour at times, though she's quite harmless. Competent psychiatric treatment could have done nothing but good and, for her own sake, ought to have been tried. But it wasn't.'

'Do you think . . .' Margaret hesitated.

'Well? Do I think what?'

'That Doña Leandra *is* harmless?'

'You mean could she have been responsible for Felipe's morphine injection and your drugged coffee?'

'Yes, I suppose I did mean that,' Margaret confessed. 'But she was the one who warned me . . . the day I

arrived, she sent for me, before I'd even seen Felipe . . .'
She told him of her strange interview with the old
Marquesa, and he listened, frowning.

'On the face of it,' he said, when she had finished, 'it
seems highly improbable, doesn't it? She would hardly
warn you, if she intended harm to the boy herself.'

Margaret was forced to concede that he was right.
'But who else is there?' she asked helplessly. 'Carlos was
with us that night at the Casa Ibañez, so he couldn't have
done it. And Louise is Felipe's mother . . .'

'Yes.' Julian's mouth tightened. 'Louise is Felipe's
mother, poor soul. You realise, of course, that the whole
thing could have been an accident? Nurse Riardos *could*
have been careless. We shan't know whether she was
until Carlos finds her—he was going to her lodgings
again today, incidentally, to see if she's returned,
and—'

'Nurse Riardos couldn't have drugged my coffee,'
Margaret put in, unanswerably, 'and she wouldn't have
drugged her own. Or'—she faced him squarely—'your
whisky, Julian.'

'*If* they were drugged, Margaret.'

'It was more than just a coincidence that we all three
fell asleep that night,' Margaret told him, with conviction.

'Perhaps,' he allowed. Then, increasing his speed, he
let his hand rest for an instant on her arm. 'I didn't bring
you out this afternoon in order to talk about this real or
imagined threat to Felipe, Margaret. Let's forget it for a
while, shall we? There are so many other things I'd
rather talk to you about.'

Margaret abandoned the topic with relief, but,
although they ceased to talk about it, it remained in the
back of her mind, a ceaseless, nagging torment.

Even when, reaching the lovely little coastal village of
Castello Delmonte, they changed into swimsuits and
went hand in hand into the cool blue water of the bay,
she could not wholly forget it, and Felipe's small, pale

face seemed to leap out to meet her as she plunged into the sparkling breakers.

Later, as the sunlight slowly faded, they flung themselves down on the still warm sand and lay, wrapped about in a companionable silence, to let the water drip off them. In the brief swimming trunks he had donned, Julian looked tanned and fit, and, glancing at him covertly from beneath her lashes, Margaret wondered how—less than a week ago—she could possibly have thought him forbidding and unapproachable. Or, for that matter, how she could have believed that she disliked him. She was very conscious of his nearness and of his arm, thrust out in front of him, touching hers. It was still damp from his swim, the bronzed skin cool, and once again she felt a tiny thrill pass through her at the contact.

He turned suddenly on his side, as if aware of her eyes on him, and reached for her hand. Propping himself on one elbow, he looked down into her face, his own eyes very bright.

'Margaret,' he said softly, 'I have so much I want to tell you. I wish we were alone.'

Her heart echoed his wish and she knew, although he made no other move to touch her, how close to each other they had come.

Julian's fingers clasped hers tightly. A family party came to sit nearby; a boy and girl, their bodies burnt almost black by the sun, raced past them, laughing together, as they made for the water. But no one was watching them and he lifted her hand to lay it against his cheek and she felt his lips, very gently, against her palm.

'The first time I ever saw you,' he said, his voice a little muffled, 'was when you'd just taken charge of my theatre, Margaret. You were very much on your dignity that day—we were both new to our responsibilities. It was my first day as a St Ninian's consultant and yours as a Sister, wasn't it?'

'I think it was. I was rather frightened of you, I remember.'

He laughed. 'And I of you! You were efficiency personified and very beautiful and aloof, and nothing I did was right for you, so I decided to take you down a peg, to see if you were human. No, wait'—as Margaret attempted indignantly to interrupt him—'let me have my say. I succeeded almost too well, I'm afraid—you thought I was criticising you and that I was difficult and temperamental and out to find fault with the whole theatre staff, and so you paid me back in my own coin. I thought you were wonderful . . . and then someone told me you were tied up with David Fellowes.' He sighed. 'I knew rather too much about that young man, my dear, for the idea to please me. Or perhaps, even then, I was jealous.'

'*Jealous?* But—' Margaret sat up, scattering the sand.

He said quietly, 'Yes, jealous, darling—didn't you know? I fell in love with you that very first day, in the theatre. And I've endured tortures ever since because, after Louise, I vowed I'd never fall in love again . . . at least not seriously, and that I'd never marry. So I fought against falling in love with you. I fought like hell, but it wasn't any use.' He caught her fiercely to him. 'I even tried, when we first got here, to put the clock back . . . Louise wanted it too because she was lonely and unhappy. That first evening, when you came upon us without warning, Margaret, she broke down and wept in my arms and we both tried then. But it was dead, so dead that it could never be resurrected. I kissed her, and it didn't mean a thing to either of us, except, perhaps, that it laid the ghost of the past, once and for ever, for her as well as for me. Her heart is with José and I think it always will be. And mine . . .'

Margaret caught her breath. 'And yours, Julian?'

'Mine belongs to you,' he told her huskily, 'if you want it. If your ghost is laid too . . . is he, Margaret?'

'I told you he was, a long time ago.'

'Yes, you did. But I wouldn't let myself believe you. I'm a jealous man, darling, and a selfish and possessive one. Will you be able to stand me? As I used to be in the theatre, I'll probably be a difficult, temperamental husband, always criticising and finding fault . . . but I do love you and I'll do my best to improve and everything in my power to make you happy. If that's enough. Do you think it will be?'

'I think it will, Julian.' Laughter bubbled in her throat, although there were tears in her eyes. 'After all, I did manage to cope with your temperament at St Ninian's, didn't I? We never actually came to blows.'

His rare smile lit his face with sudden tenderness. In the fading light on the beach, the others who shared it with them had become shadowy, indistinct figures, without substance or reality, and they were isolated now in a small, lost world of their own. Julian took her hands and drew her up beside him. His lips found hers and they clung together for a timeless moment in eager, breathless ecstasy. Then, reluctantly, he released her.

'We'll have to go, darling. It's getting late.'

'Yes, I know. I *wish* we didn't have to go.'

'I too, my love. But we'll come again and there will be other places to see together—not only now but for the rest of our lives. Don't forget that . . . there'll be the whole world, when you're my wife, Margaret.'

That promise buoyed her up, and her step was light when she left him by the row of small, gaily painted beach huts and went in search of the one in which she had changed. She dressed quickly, anxious to rejoin him, but he was waiting for her when she returned to the car. When he had started the car, he reached for her hand and tucked it into the crook of his arm.

They spoke little during the drive back, but Margaret, sitting there in the warm, pine-scented darkness with Julian at her side, was conscious of the greatest happiness she had ever known in her life. She let her head fall on to his shoulder, intending only to let it rest there for an instant, but he said gruffly, when she moved, 'No, stay where you are . . . and sleep if you want to, darling. As you did on the flight over, remember? You almost unnerved me then, I wanted so much to kiss you. But instead I flung Fellowes in your face, didn't I, and bullied and reproached you. You must have hated me!'

'I did,' Margaret told him sleepily, and then, drowsy from the swim and the mountain air, she relaxed against him and slept, as he had bidden her, feeling the firm, even beat of his heart against her cheek.

She didn't wake until they were slowing down outside the lodge gates.

Carlos met them on the steps leading up to the front door. He said, without preamble, 'Well, I have found Nurse Riardos at last. But I fear it is not going to help us a great deal.'

'Why isn't it?' Julian demanded.

Carlos' dark eyes were angry. 'Because,' he answered grimly, 'she met with an accident after she left here—a car knocked her down in the street and she was taken to hospital. I have been there, but I was not permitted to see her. She is not seriously hurt but'—he shrugged—'she has concussion, the doctor in charge told me, and she remembers nothing. He thinks it will be several days before she is able to remember anything that happened before her accident.'

Julian's gaze met Margaret's in swift dismay and she knew that the ordeal was not yet over. But at least she and Julian would be facing it together. She wasn't alone, she thought thankfully. She heard him ask Carlos how his mother was and then followed him up the wide, gracefully curving staircase to the old lady's bedroom as the front door closed, with finality, behind them.

CHAPTER ELEVEN

MARGARET paid two visits to Doña Leandra during the night, carefully locking Felipe's door before leaving him and taking the key with her.

On her first visit, she found the old lady sleeping peacefully, a huddled, infinitely pathetic little figure in the enormous, old-fashioned four-poster with its brocade hangings and the beautiful satin quilt. Sleep had robbed her of much of her normal dignity, and, in the absence of the familiar black *mantilla*, her snowy hair looked sparse and untidy, her face—surprisingly like Felipe's in repose—much less forbidding. The skin was the colour of old parchment and stretched so tightly over the high de Fontera cheekbones that it seemed almost transparent.

Doña Leandra was a de Fontera both by birth and by marriage, since she had married a second cousin, and Margaret wondered, looking down at the still, shuttered face, what secrets it hid and what dreams and hopes and fears were concealed behind the mask-like calm it now displayed to her searching eyes.

What had the old Marquesa meant by her strange, insistent warning? What purpose lay behind it and what had it achieved? She herself had not taken it seriously to begin with, and now, looking back, the fact that it had been delivered at all added to, rather than detracted from her suspicions, made her search in her mind for some ulterior motive which would account for it.

She bent and lifted one thin, long-fingered hand from the coverlet, feeling for a pulse. It was remarkably strong and regular for a woman of Doña Leandra's age and apparently frail physique, and her breathing, although shallow, was steady and even. There was, Margaret decided, no cause for anxiety here. As Julian had said, after his last examination, Doña Leandra appeared to have made an extraordinarily rapid recovery and to have suffered few ill-effects from her sudden attack.

She returned, moving on tip-toe down the long, dimly lit corridor, to her own patient, reassured by the sight of Julian's half-open door, as she passed it.

On her second visit to Doña Leandra's room, just before dawn, Margaret found the old lady awake, drinking coffee from a flask which María had left by her bedside. Without being given the chance to explain her presence, she was subjected to a swift and withering attack.

'What are you doing here, Miss?' Doña Leandra demanded furiously. 'Is not your place with my grandson, the little Don Felipe? Go back at once . . . at once, I say! Don Felipe is not to be left alone.'

'I came to make certain that you were all right, *señora*,' Margaret told her, as soon as she could interrupt the tirade. She moved towards the bed, reaching for the sick woman's wrist, but Doña Leandra jerked her hand away with surprising strength.

'Of course I am all right! I do not need you for anything. If I require assistance, I can ring for María, can I not? It is her duty to serve me, not yours. Return to your post immediately when you are told. Who knows what, in your absence from his side, may have befallen my grandson?'

'It's unlikely that anything can have befallen him, Doña Leandra. I have been here for less than five minutes, and, in any case, the door to his room is locked and I have the key in my pocket.' Margaret held it up. 'See, here it is.'

But Doña Leandra refused to be mollified. 'He could have choked in his sleep . . . or wakened to find himself alone. Children are afraid of the dark, as you, who are supposedly trained in these matters, should be aware.'

'He isn't in the dark, there is a light burning in his room. And Mr Freyton is next door, so if Felipe wakes and is frightened, he has only to call out. Please, Doña Leandra, let me take your tray away and make you comfortable. It's not even daylight yet and you should try to sleep a little longer.'

'I can sleep without your help. Take my tray, if you must. I have finished with it.' The black eyes gleamed dangerously as Doña Leandra thrust the tray in Margaret's direction. But her old hands were clumsy in their impatience. The cup she had been drinking from slid across the polished wooden surface of her bedside table, spilling its contents on the lacy sleeve of her nightgown, and she held her arm up indignantly. 'Now, see the mess you have made with your interference!'

'I'm very sorry. I'll get you a clean nightgown at once, Doña Leandra, and a bowl of water for you to wash your hands in. There . . .' Margaret mopped industriously at the table-top. 'It won't take long.'

'It is to be hoped that it will not,' Doña Leandra returned, her voice icy. 'My nightgowns are kept in that closet, in one of the lower drawers, I think.'

Margaret went into the adjoining bathroom, filled a bowl with warm water and brought it, with soap and a towel, to the bedside. She left Doña Leandra, who was complaining fretfully at the delay, to wash the coffee-stains from her hands, and crossed to the large clothes-closet, on the opposite side of the room, in search of a fresh nightgown. The first drawer she opened contained underclothing, all handmade and of the finest cambric, packed neatly away with lavender bags between each layer of clothing. There were, however, no nightgowns, and she opened a second drawer and then a third. Like the first, each was packed to capacity, and, delving beneath the top layer, Margaret's fingers encountered a small object that felt cold to the touch. Surprised, she took it out and saw that it was a key. She stared at it in the palm of her hand for a moment or two, wondering why it seemed familiar and then, with a sense of acute shock, realised that it was exactly the size and shape of the one Nurse Riardos was supposed to have mislaid . . . the key which, originally, had unlocked the drawer in Felipe's room in which the drugs were kept.

'You are being very slow, *señorita*,' Doña Leandra informed her acidly, and Margaret hurriedly picked up one of the folded nightgowns and laid it on the bed.

'Let me help you, Doña Leandra,' she offered. Almost as an afterthought, she slipped the key she had found into the pocket of her overall. She couldn't be certain that it *was* the missing key, but, if she tried it in the drawer and it fitted, then . . . Margaret caught her breath sharply. If not the complete proof they sought, it would at least be a pointer, and, if she told Julian, he . . .

'*Señorita*,' Doña Leandra said plaintively, 'have you not wasted enough time?'

Margaret picked up the nightgown, her hands not quite steady. When the old lady had been helped into it and her pillows straightened, Margaret took her leave, a parting injunction not to return ringing in her ears. She found Julian at his door when she went back to the sickroom. Holding out his hand to her, he asked, 'Is everything all right, Margaret? I heard you go, and then, when you didn't come back, I wondered if old Doña Leandra . . .' He broke off at the sight of her expression. 'Darling, what is it?'

Margaret took his hand, glad for a moment of its support. 'Doña Leandra is all right. But I found *this* in one of her drawers.' She offered the key for his inspection and added unhappily, 'As a matter of fact, it was hidden in one of her drawers, Julian, and I only found it by chance.'

He looked down at the small, bright object, brows coming together in a thoughtful pucker. 'I don't recognise it,' he confessed, 'but I take it you're trying to tell me it's the missing key—the one Riardos is supposed to have gone off with?'

'I can't tell for certain until I try it in the lock, but it *looks* like the one.'

'Is that so?' He sighed and pulled his dressing gown closer about him. 'Well, come on.' His tone was regretful, as if what he were about to do went very much against the grain. 'We'll have to try it, I suppose. But if it fits . . . what then, Margaret?'

'I don't know,' she answered helplessly, and stepped past him to open Felipe's door. He took the small, bright key she had found from her unresisting hand and they crossed the room together. As Margaret had feared it would, the key fitted the lock of the now empty drug cupboard perfectly, and her heart was heavy as she looked up into Julian's eyes.

He said resignedly, 'You were right, darling. I shall have to think about what we must do . . . perhaps if I have a word with García he'll be able to suggest something. She's not responsible for her actions, of course—in the legal sense, that is.'

'No, of course not.'

He shrugged. 'There's one good thing about it, my darling. You won't have to worry any more, when you're alone at night with Felipe, will you? Now that we *know*.'

Margaret felt a lump rise in her throat. She was about to turn away when Julian put his arm round her, holding her to him. He didn't speak, but she sensed his distress and realised that it transcended her own.

'Will you tell Louise?' she asked miserably.

'I shall have to, darling. She's got to know, so that she can take what steps are necessary to safeguard Felipe. It must not be allowed to happen again.'

Margaret knew that he was right: It was something that had to be done, and, remembering what Carlos had told her about the accidents Felipe had suffered during his childhood, she shivered. Feeling it, Julian's arms tightened about her.

'Does the key really prove it was Doña Leandra?' she questioned uncertainly.

'Well, it's not the sort of proof a court of law would accept. But if you consider motive and opportunity and the fact that the old lady is undoubtedly senile, then I imagine it's enough.' He put two fingers beneath her chin, lifting her face to his and studying it for a moment or two before kissing her gently. 'You don't want to believe it was Doña Leandra, do you, Margaret?'

She shook her head. Autocratic and irascible though the old lady was, she could not bear to think that old Doña Leandra could have been responsible for the attempts on Felipe's life. The boy was fond of his grandmother, and when he was well, Pilar had told her, he spent much of his time in her company, reading aloud to her, walking with her in the grounds, talking to her . . . It was dreadful to think that, for the sake of his own safety, he could not be allowed to do so again.

'Julian, couldn't we wait, just for a few more days, to make absolutely certain? If we were wrong, just think what it would do to that poor old lady . . . and to Felipe too. And while she's in bed, confined to her room—what danger could there be? We can be on our guard, we can take care that she's never left alone in here with him. But if you speak to Dr García and if you tell the Marquesa, she'd have to be taken away, wouldn't she? Perhaps she might have to be certified.'

'It's possible,' Julian conceded.

'Well, then . . . couldn't we wait, until we're sure?'

'How do we make sure?' he countered wearily. 'By using Felipe to bait a trap?'

'No, if you put it like that, we can't, of course.'

He laid his cheek on hers. 'You're a sentimental child, darling. You know as well as I do that I shall have to tell Dr García. He's the family doctor, it would be quite unethical to withold all knowledge of this from him, in the circumstances.'

She couldn't argue. Obviously Dr García would have

to be told. Julian smiled at her. 'Try to forget about it, my love. I'm going back to bed now, to catch up on some of the sleep I haven't had, and this time, thank heaven, I shan't have to sleep with one ear open, listening for you or Felipe to call out.' He looked tired, Margaret realised pityingly, as she lifted her face for his kiss. Tired and . . . disillusioned. The secret they had uncovered was not a pleasant one, and as she walked with him to the door, she found herself wishing that she hadn't discovered the missing key.

But it was too late for regrets now. She *had* discovered it, and it pointed, unerringly it seemed, to Doña Leandra. As she returned to her chair at Felipe's bedside, she remembered the state in which she had found him, after her visit to Barcélona with Carlos, and as she remembered, her resolution hardened. Doña Leandra might be old and senile and heartbroken, but what she had tried to do couldn't be excused. Julian had accused her of being sentimental . . . she bit back a sigh. Perhaps she was. But her first loyalty must be to Felipe. He was her patient and he had to be protected, whatever the pity she might feel for the poor, unhappy old woman who had schemed to put her own son in his place.

The remainder of Margaret's duty passed quietly and without incident. Felipe was in the highest of spirits when he wakened, and when Sister Teresa reported for duty, Margaret left them laughing happily together over some private joke of their own, which appeared to afford them both the greatest amusement. Normally she would have tried to share it with them, but this morning she found it was beyond her even to smile.

Julian breakfasted with her in the balcony room overlooking the fountain, and they arranged to meet at four, in order to drive into Barcelona together to visit the cathedral. Breakfast over, Margaret took leave of him and retired to her own room to sleep.

And this became, for the next week, the pattern of their days. Each evening Julian took her sightseeing with him, and the hours she spent in his company were the happiest she had ever known. Together, like any other tourists, they explored the dark, winding streets and palaces of medieval Barcelona, losing sight of the sun in its maze of closely built old houses and torturously twisting alleyways. They climbed down to inspect the excavations which had uncovered part of the lost Roman fortress and, emerging into the modern world again, mounted the steps leading from the Plaza del Rey to the great hall of the palace of the Counts of Barcelona. They visited art galleries and the museum on the sea-front which housed the relics of Columbus, with its scale-model replica of his tiny flagship, the *Santa María*. They ascended by lift to the top of the column and, standing beneath the vast statue of the discoverer of America, gazed entranced across the roof-tops of the city to the distant hills.

In the cool of the evening, their sightseeing over, they strolled about the Flower Market or sat, quietly sipping cups of fragrant coffee and watching the passers-by, in one of the many gay little awning-shaded cafés which lined the *Ramblas*. They were content simply because they were with each other and deeply in love. Julian bought her roses, filling her arms with them, and for Margaret these were golden, enchanted hours, precious and never to be forgotten, because he had made them so and because they were cut off completely from their other life, at St Ninian's and with the de Fonteras.

Their promised visit to Montserrat came at the end of the week and was, for both of them, the highlight of their stay. Julian's return to London was looming very close now, and Margaret dreaded the thought of his going, and was tempted to give up her own planned holiday—which was to come when Felipe no longer needed her—in order to cut short their separation.

But Julian would not hear of it. He had other plans, he told her, but, smiling mysteriously, refused to disclose what these were until, as he put it, the time was ripe.

Felipe was continuing to make excellent progress, and, despite the discomfort of his plaster, he was cheerfully and courageously patient. His mother saw more of him than she had done since the operation, but the habit of years was not easy to break and her efforts to bridge the gulf between them were fraught with many disappointments on both sides. Louise de Fontera tried hard, but she was uncertain in her approach to the boy, and Felipe himself was over-eager at one moment and shy and withdrawn the next, which did not help her. He was not accustomed to having his mother make a fuss of him and, childlike, he clung to those he felt he could trust—to Sister Teresa, María, Margaret herself and, pathetically, to his grandmother, for whom he was constantly asking.

Doña Leandra remained in her own room. Julian had spoken to Dr García, Margaret knew, but the old doctor was a Spaniard and he held the de Fontera family in some awe and was reluctant to take any positive action, one way or the other. He showed a genius for procrastination; he made excuses, fell back on the Spanish pretext of *mañana*, waiting to see what the morrow would bring. He argued, spread his hands in despair and, in the end, did nothing. On his insistence, neither Louise nor Carlos de Fontera was told of these suspicions, and he would not allow the old lady herself to be questioned at all.

'There is time,' he said obstinately. 'You cannot be certain that you are right, and only time will show if you are. It is better to wait, to watch Doña Leandra carefully and to say nothing to her which might alarm her. If she is the one, she will betray herself, sooner or later. If she is not and you have accused her falsely, irreparable harm might be done. Don Carlos would undoubtedly take offence. In the meantime, she is ill and must be permitted to rest.'

While there was the excuse of her heart condition to justify keeping her in bed, Dr García kept her there, but when she insisted, he allowed her to get up and sit in a chair, so long as she did not leave her bedroom.

She had her own nurse in the daytime, and at night Margaret continued to keep her under supervision. Doña Leandra did not like her doing so, but when pleas, protests and even commands failed to have the desired effect, she submitted with a better grace than Margaret had expected her to display and seemed, towards the latter part of the week, even to welcome her visits. She never admitted that she was pleased to see the British girl, but she delayed her coffee-drinking until Margaret appeared, and then, making the excuse that María had left her a larger flask than she needed for herself, would insist on their sharing it.

The old lady slept badly and, during the little ceremony she made of their nightly repast, she liked to talk. Her conversation was more of days gone by than of the present, for much of the time her mind dwelt in the past and she frequently spoke of her eldest son as if he were still alive. She talked sometimes of Felipe, but never mentioned her son's widow or, indeed, admitted that she was aware of his marriage.

Listening to her, Margaret felt like a traitor and deliberately tried to forget what she was told. She did not repeat it, even to Julian, and he, wisely, did not question her. She felt ashamed of her own suspicions. On the first occasion when old Doña Leandra poured her a cup of coffee from her flask, she had tried to refuse it and, being overruled, had drunk it cautiously, a sip at a time, savouring each mouthful and finally putting down her cup still half full. But she had suffered no ill effects from it; there had been no repetition of the sensation of terrifying lassitude that had come over her on the night of Felipe's collapse. Now, feeling still more ashamed, she drank what she was given without betraying any open hesitation, and as her acquaintance with her patient's grandmother ripened into something approaching friendship, she came bitterly to regret her discovery of the key and everything that had resulted from it.

Julian, understanding her better than she knew, begged her not to relax her caution.

The evening before he was due to leave for London, he took her back to Castello Delmonte. Sister Teresa had kindly offered to extend her normal hours of duty until ten, to enable them to have a meal together before Margaret relieved her, and with so many hours of freedom stretching before her, Margaret did her best to enjoy them.

The small, treé-ringed beach was as lovely as she remembered it, the sun as bright, the water as sparkling and crystal-clear as it had been the first time they had come here. Because it was the place where Julian had proposed to her, her memories of it were locked in her heart, and as she changed in the tiny, red-painted wooden cabin, she tried to recapture those memories and the joy she had felt. But, for all her efforts, she could not do so. A heaviness lay over her spirit, which was not only caused by the imminence of Julian's departure, and when she ran across the warm golden sand to meet him, although she forced a smile, she knew that he was aware of it.

He caught her hand, holding her to him for an instant, and then, shortening his long stride to match hers, he ran with her to meet the lazily incoming tide. The shallow water was crowded with people, all carefree and laughing, but, swimming with long, powerful strokes, Julian led her after him until only a suntanned boy on a water-bicycle was in earshot—and he was pedalling slowly back towards the beach. Soon they had outdistanced him and Julian rolled over on to his back, putting out a hand to draw her level with him.

'Margaret,' he said gently, 'there's something bothering you, isn't there? And it's not entirely because I have to leave that you're worried.'

Margaret, breathless from her swim, didn't at once

reply. Then, wretchedly, she admitted that his guess was correct.

'Well?' he urged, 'what is it? You mustn't keep things from me, darling, if they worry you. I think I have the right to know, don't you?'

'Of course you have. And I'd tell you, if it were anything I could put into words. Only it's not, it's . . . oh, it's just a vague sort of instinctive feeling that we've let ourselves be deceived and that we're on the wrong track.'

'You mean'—he trod water, coming closer to her so that he could see her face—'you mean that we're wrong about old Doña Leandra?'

'Yes, I suppose that's what I do mean. But I can't offer you any very convincing arguments to prove my point, I'm afraid. I wish I could. As I told you, it's more instinctive than reasoned.'

'They always say that a woman's intuition is to be relied on, darling.'

'You're not taking me seriously,' Margaret reproached him.

'On the contrary,' he assured her soberly, 'I'm taking you very seriously indeed. I always have, you know. Do you feel very strongly that we're wrong?'

'Yes,' she said, 'I do, Julian.'

'Right, we'll take that as read, then. I may say that old Dr Garcia shares your belief, but he hasn't any very convincing reasons for it either. He just says he's known the old lady for a long time and that it's completely out of character.'

'It *is*!' Margaret put in eagerly. 'I've got to know her better since she's been ill. Oh, I'm not pretending that I know her well—she isn't easy to know and she's very proud, she keeps one at a distance. But she talks to me quite a lot at night, when I look in to see how she is. We drink coffee together. The last two nights, she's kept me with her for about half an hour and—'

'Do you still lock Felipe's door?' Julian asked quickly.

'No, I stopped doing it after we found the drug cupboard key. There seemed no point after that. But last night I locked it again.'

'Why? Because of your instinctive belief in Doña Leandra's innocence?'

'I suppose it was partly that. But I knew I'd be gone longer than I felt it was safe to leave Felipe alone.'

Julian turned on to his back again. The buoyancy of the water kept both of them easily afloat and Margaret closed her eyes against the glare of the sun. It was very peaceful, and she felt her tension gradually relax until Julian said suddenly, breaking the silence which had fallen between them, 'I'd go on locking that door, darling—especially after I leave.'

She thought of the confidence that having him so close at hand had always given her, and wished, for the thousandth time, that he did not have to go. But obviously he had to; they had gone into it all before—he had his practice to attend to, his work at St Ninian's to do, and he had only arranged to be away for a fortnight. He couldn't stay on. But *she* had to, she had promised that she would, and in any case, until the threat to Felipe was removed, she couldn't desert him.

Julian said, reading her unvoiced thoughts, 'Margaret, my darling, if you want to change your mind and come back with me, I think it could be arranged, you know. Even now, at the eleventh hour.'

For a moment Margaret was tempted, but then she thought of Felipe and her resolution hardened. 'My job here isn't finished, is it, Julian? My patient still needs me.'

'Yes,' he conceded reluctantly, 'but if you're afraid . . . this isn't your battle, you know.'

'But Felipe's my patient, darling. Doesn't that make it my battle?'

He came closer to her and she felt his arms go round her fiercely. 'I *hate* to leave you, Margaret—in these circumstances particularly, it's almost more than I can do.' He gestured to the distant beach. 'Let's go back, shall we? I'm going to ring up Peter Cahill and ask him if he can carry on for another week. There's a telephone at the beach café. If I can get a call through now, I might just catch him before he leaves Harley Street.'

'But, Julian—' Margaret began. 'You can't . . .'

'Can't I?' Julian returned firmly. 'You see if I can't, my love! Although . . .' he sighed, and his smile was rueful as he added, 'I *had* planned to get Peter to do a locum for me when your holiday starts, in three weeks' time. I thought, if you were agreeable, that we might get ourselves married here and have your holiday as our honeymoon.'

'Was that the plan you weren't going to tell me about, until the time was ripe?' Margaret asked, oddly moved.

'It was, darling. But the best laid plans . . . oh well, that's what happens, isn't it? I'd even worked out what I was going to say to your mother and father, in order to persuade them to dispense with a white wedding in London for you. In fact . . .'

'Couldn't we stick to that plan?' Margaret interrupted, her throat tight.

He brushed water from his eyes, his smile widening.

'It appeals to you?'

'Yes, it . . . does.'

'Oh, Margaret!' He laid his cheek against hers. 'If you only knew how much I love you, darling! But it's far *too* much to enable me to leave you here if you're likely to be in any danger. I'm sorry, but it is. Come on.' He released her and struck off for the beach. 'Let's get it over with, shall we?'

The call to London took longer to put through than either of them had expected, despite the assistance of the café proprietor and his two pretty daughters, who were intrigued and anxious to help. When, eventually, Julian's secretary answered, it was to say that Peter Cahill had been called to the hospital for an emergency operation and the most she could promise was that she would ask him to ring Julian at the de Fonteras' house later in the evening.

'That's cutting it rather fine,' Julian complained, 'but I suppose there's nothing else we can do. Well'—he smiled down into Margaret's upturned face—'we've a couple of hours before we need start back, and if Peter telephones before that, someone will take a message. Miss Leedham will tell him what I want, she understands exactly, but failing all else, I'll fly back tonight, as arranged, fix up another locum as quickly as I can and then come back. That's about the best I can do, darling. In the meantime, since this may be our last evening together for a while, let's enjoy it, shall we? Where would you like to eat?'

Margaret looked round the small, unpretentious café uncertainly. The proprietor, meeting her gaze, gave her a little bow.

'We are serving very good food here, *señor* ... *señorita*. Fine sea-food ... *zarzuela de mariscos, changurros, merluza, calamares*, you have only to choose and I will cook for you what you will. We have dance orchestra also,' he added hopefully.

'Well?' Julian asked.

'Let's stay, darling. They've been awfully nice to us over our telephoning.'

Julian laughed. 'Because they were nice about the telephone, you're prepared to risk an indifferent meal, simply to repay them. Margaret, you're wonderful! But I love you for it, all the same. Come on, let's sit over by the window and we'll have some wine while we're waiting. At least that's likely to be reasonable, even if the rest isn't.'

But, contrary to his gloomy prophecies, the meal proved to be excellent, and the dance orchestra, although it consisted of three shabby young musicians in jeans and faded shirts, made up in enthusiasm for what it lacked in skill, and, their meal over, they danced to it happily. It was too early for many Spaniards to eat dinner, but a number of British and American tourists followed them into the café, and when it was time for them to leave, the little place was full, with everyone having the time of their lives. The plump little proprietor presented his modest bill and bowed them out of his restaurant and they left it with regret, promising to come again.

They drove back, the moon shining silver in the purple backcloth of sky and a galaxy of stars gleaming brightly, as if in token of good fortune. Julian sang softly as he drove and Margaret sat dazed with the magnitude of her happiness and the love she felt for him. It didn't seem possible that their parting could be so near, and as they turned once more into the drive gates, acknowledging the lodge-keeper's salute, she found herself praying that it need not come tonight. They drew nearer to the great house that was Felipe's, and as it came into view at a bend in the drive, ablaze with lights, a dreadful foreboding seized her, a premonition of what was to come. But she would not speak of it to Julian, chiding herself for a fool who had let her imagination run away with her. Nothing had changed, the house was just the same . . . it was simply, because Julian might be leaving it, that she felt afraid. Her fears had done the rest, she told herself, as she followed him into the hall.

The major-domo gave him a message, carefully written down on a slip of paper. Julian read it and turned, his mouth tightly compressed, to Margaret.

'I'm sorry . . .' She guessed what he was about to say and forced herself to smile at him, as he told her that Peter Cahill had made other plans and couldn't possibly change them at such short notice. 'He says that if he can later on, he will, darling. But I'm afraid it'll be too late. My plane leaves at midnight, so I shall have to go. Take care of yourself, Margaret. Promise me you'll take care of yourself!'

Their farewell, with the major-domo hovering attentively in the background, was brief and deceptively casual. Margaret went up to her room to change into uniform, while Julian took his leave of Louise and Carlos de Fontera.

He came, for a moment, to the sickroom before he left, and as Margaret listened to his footsteps receding down the long corridor, a sense of desolation swept over her. But she went about her work, grimly determined not to allow herself to yield to it. The sound of a car engine starting up outside told her that Julian was on the point of departure; it faded into silence a few minutes afterwards and she knew then that he had gone.

She busied herself with routine tasks, but Felipe was sleeping soundly and there was little for her to do. After she had paid her first visit to Doña Leandra's room and found her asleep also, she returned to Felipe's bedside, and, sitting down in her chair, attempted to read.

María came in with her tray of sandwiches and a flask of coffee as usual at midnight. When the maid had gone, she poured out a cup and swallowed it, scarcely aware of what she was drinking, save that it was black and very strong.

And then, to her horror, the nightmare she had endured before started again. She became aware of a dreadful tiredness creeping over her, knew again the heaviness of brain and body, the struggle for breath that had come to her the night after Felipe's operation. Once more she fought against the overpowering desire for sleep, felt her eyelids close and somehow frantically forced them open again. She searched for the bell, as she had done before and managed, this time, to ring it.

Then, remembering the door, she groped her way to it through the inky, impenetrable darkness that was closing about her, her fingers clawing at its smoothly polished surface in a last, desperate endeavour to find the key and turn it.

But the key wasn't in the lock. It took a minute or two for this fact to penetrate to her numbed brain, and when it did, Margaret sank back on her heels with a little sob

Her fear grew until it became a living thing, tearing at her unmercifully as she waged her futile, losing battle against the longing to sleep.

She tried to drag herself to her feet, grasping the door handle for support, and, to her stunned dismay, she felt it turn in her hand.

Someone was outside, in the corridor, someone who sought admission, stealthily and secretly, to the room in which Felipe slept.

From a long, long way away a voice whispered her name, and she recognised it with a stab of horror, for it was the last voice she had expected to hear.

CHAPTER TWELVE

'ARE you there, Miss Hay? Are you still awake?'

Margaret heard the whisper, but she couldn't answer it. She slipped back on to her knees, and the door, free now of her weight against it, was opened cautiously.

Louise de Fontera came in smiling. She saw Margaret and went to her, reaching with a disdainful hand for her wrist. But her pulse-taking was professionally competent, and so was the manner in which, a moment later, she lifted the younger girl's eyelids and looked into her eyes.

'Not quite off yet?' she suggested dispassionately. 'Well, it shouldn't take long. The sleeping tablets which the good Dr García prescribes for me are very effective and I made sure that you were given an adequate dose. But I'm afraid you aren't going to wake up this time, Margaret Hay . . . neither you nor Felipe. It's a pity, I'd have spared you if I could, but I have to make it look like an accident, you see.'

She bent and, with surprising strength, lifted Margaret to her feet. 'Come on,' she ordered impatiently, 'you can walk, can't you? Help me to get you over to that chair.'

Margaret attempted to resist her, but it was no use. Her limbs were like lead and she couldn't control them. Half dragging, half carrying her, Louise got her to the chair at Felipe's bedside and she collapsed into it, fighting desperately to retain her senses.

Louise de Fontera went over to the bed. She bent over her son and, to Margaret's shocked bewilderment, kissed him tenderly. She said, in a voice that shook with emotion, 'Forgive me, my darling, but it will be better for you this way. You won't have to suffer any more, you won't have any more pain, and no one will laugh at you or despise you because you're not like other boys . . .' Her hand touched Felipe's sleeping face, smoothing back an unruly lock of dark hair that had fallen across his forehead. In the shaded light from the bedside lamp, the enormous solitaire diamond on her finger glittered and sparkled as her hand moved. Looking from it to her face, Margaret saw that her eyes were full of tears, which shone in their blue depths as brightly as the diamond.

She was mad, the girl thought despairingly, there could be no other explanation. And yet, strangely, she loved Felipe. She—who had sought to take his life—had done so for no other reason. She had nothing to gain from his death and everything to lose, but she was prepared, in spite of this, to bring it about because she believed that it was for the boy's sake, to spare him suffering.

Evidently she hadn't accepted Julian's assurance or her own that the operation had been a success. Her mind, twisted and tormented beyond endurance by the long years of loneliness, had been unable to take it in, and even her training hadn't been proof against her fear that, for Felipe, there was no cure.

This knowledge, coming to her at such a moment, added to the nightmare quality of Margaret's thoughts. She tried to speak, to cry out, but her words, when they came, were slurred and without meaning. And Louise de Fontera, in any case, wasn't listening. She straightened and braced herself, scarcely sparing Margaret a glance. Then she crossed to the fireplace and, dropping swiftly to her knees before the gas fire, turned on the tap which supplied it from a portable cylinder in the hearth.

The fire had been installed, Margaret recalled miserably, when preparations were being made for Felipe's operation to be performed in the house. Nurse Riardos had pointed it out to her, with the suggestion that it might be useful on night duty, but the nights had been too warm for her to have needed it and so the cylinder was probably full. Listening to the hiss of escaping gas, she again attempted to speak, but only a small whimper came from between her parted lips, and Louise ignored it.

'They'll think,' she said aloud, 'that you lit the fire and let it blow out, won't they? There's a breeze, and if I leave the window open a little, it will seem quite plausible.' She addressed her words to Margaret but didn't look at her. 'This was what I meant to do the first time, you know, after you'd spoilt everything by coming back from Carlos' party too soon. I crept in, but you didn't hear me, you were asleep. I turned on the tap, but the fools hadn't connected the cylinder properly and nothing happened. I locked you in, too, and took the tray away, so that no one would suspect anything. This time I won't lock you in, because it might be questioned, but I'll leave the key in the lock, as you left it, and I must remember to take the coffee tray when I go. I'm sorry'— she came to stand looking down at Margaret now—'to have to do this to you, for Julian's sake. He's very much in love with you, poor Julian! And I owe him a great deal, he's always been kind to me . . . and to Felipe, although he couldn't cure him, could he?' She leaned closer, peering intently into Margaret's face. 'You're listening, aren't you?' she demanded. 'You can hear what I'm saying to you?'

Margaret struggled vainly to ward off the black, suffocating clouds that were closing about her, but it was useless. Her eyelids were too heavy for her to lift them, and her body, slumped in the chair, no longer felt as if it were part of her. She couldn't answer Louise's question, couldn't even plead for her own life or Felipe's. But she could still hear the hissing of the gas and the voice of the woman at her side, which was telling her, quietly and reasonably, why it was necessary for Felipe to die. Only now she couldn't take any of it in and the voice faded slowly into silence. The last words she caught were something about a lawsuit, and they were completely meaningless.

She didn't know when Louise de Fontera left the room. There was no sound of the door closing, only silence. Margaret was no longer afraid, but that, she realised, must be the effect of the drug she had taken. Her last conscious thought was that even with the size of the room and the half-open window, it wouldn't take long to accomplish Louise's purpose, if nobody came. And who was there to come? Julian was winging his way back to London, the servants were asleep, Sister Teresa would not come until morning and Carlos might be anywhere.

She breathed a little prayer for the repose of Felipe's soul and knew that she could fight no longer against the terrible, compelling urge to sleep . . .

At the airport, Julian looked anxiously at his watch. For the third time, he advanced purposefully to the public telephone operator's window, but she shook her head apologetically.

'Not yet, *señor*, I am sorry. There is a delay of half an hour on calls to London.'

'But this is urgent,' Julian told her, 'my flight is due to leave in half an hour. Please, do your best to get through for me, will you?' He laid a note on the counter, whose denomination made the girl's eyes widen. But she accepted it reluctantly. 'I shall in any case do my best for you, *señor*,' she promised. 'This isn't necessary.'

'Keep it, anyway, *señorita*. It will be worth all of that if I can get through before my flight is called.'

She thanked him prettily and he returned to his seat in the lounge. He must have been mad, he told himself savagely, not to have thought of Arnold Nickson before. Arnold had just returned from six months at Johns Hopkins in America; he hadn't yet obtained his expected consultantship and would be at a loose end in London for at least another two or three weeks. He was the obvious person to ask to take over the practice, and St Ninian's would count themselves fortunate to have his services, even for a short time. Providing, of course, that Julian could get hold of him within the next half hour. It was damnable about the delay. He had made it a person-to-person call, which might help if Arnold wasn't at his flat, but even so . . . Julian looked again at his watch and swore under his breath. It seemed half a lifetime ago that he had left Margaret, although, in fact, it was less than two hours. He got up to pace the floor restlessly. He ought never to have left her, he reproached himself.

He had teased her about her woman's intuition and her instinctive conviction that old Doña Leandra was not the person responsible for the attempt on Felipe's life, but . . . he expelled his breath in a long-drawn sigh of frustration. He, too, was acting on an instinctive conviction now. Every instinct he possessed cried out to him that Margaret had need of him, and for the first time in his life he hadn't questioned the whys and wherefores, but had acted blindly. She had done that to him, he thought, and his lips curved into a wry smile. She had made him love her more than his work or his ambitions; more, even, than life itself, and he knew, standing there staring helplessly at the row of telephone kiosks, that if his flight left before he was able to contact Arnold Nickson, he wouldn't be on it.

He had kept Ramón waiting with the car, on impulse, while he rang through to the de Fonteras' house, and even though Carlos had assured him that the house was quiet and Margaret had just paid a visit to his mother, he hadn't been satisfied. He hadn't told Ramón he could go but, instead, had asked him to wait until midnight and had tipped him well. The chauffeur would wait, he was certain, at any rate until he heard the flight called.

Perhaps, Julian thought, he had better hand in his ticket now, to save time. Then he could go straight out to the car. He would tell the reservations clerk that he was only postponing his journey. If necessary, and if he couldn't get hold of Arnold, he could take the morning flight, after he had been back to reassure himself as to Margaret's safety. He crossed to the reservations desk and had just finished his business there when he heard his name being called. He hastily thrust his papers into his pocket, and in half a dozen long, impatient strides was at the switchboard operator's window.

'Your call to London, Señor Freyton. In Box Number Three, if you please . . . Señor Nickson is on the line.'

He thanked her and dived for the box. Arnold's voice answered him, sounding a little surprised.

'Julian, old boy . . . what's this in aid of, if I may ask? I gather you're in Barcelona and . . .'

Julian cut him short. 'I am, and I want to stay here for another week. It's a matter of some urgency or I wouldn't have asked you, right out of the blue like this. But I wondered if you could possibly hold the fort for me. At my rooms and at St Ninian's . . . Peter Cahill's been doing it for a fortnight, but he can't carry on.'

'Why, of course I'll do that,' Arnold Nickson answered promptly. 'I'll be glad to, as a matter of fact—I'm a little tired of twiddling my thumbs and waiting for a nice, juicy appointment to turn up . . . which it hasn't, so far.' He asked a few pertinent questions and then, breaking into Julian's thanks, enquired mildly if he were to be let into the secret.

'Secret?' Julian echoed, and heard his colleague laugh.

'Naturally. *You* don't usually do things like this, do you? What's *cherchez la femme* in Spanish? I imagine you've got yourself involved with a dark-eyed *señorita* . . . or am I being improbably romantic?'

'Not this time,' Julian told him. 'If you want to know, I'm hoping to get married. But you'll have to wait to check up on the colour of her eyes until I bring her home. Thanks again, Arnold. I'll see you in a week.'

'Make it two if you want to,' Arnold said, and added dryly, 'Congratulations, Julian! I must say I was beginning to wonder when you'd settle down.'

Julian was smiling as he replaced his receiver, but his smile faded a moment later. Arnold couldn't possibly know the lengths he had gone to in order to make this call, he reflected. But thank heaven he'd caught him in and found him so willing to fit in with his sudden change of plan. Now he could return to Margaret with a clear conscience. He wondered if he would find, when he got back to the de Fonteras' house, that his instincts had been at fault. If they were, Margaret would probably laugh at him, but . . . his mouth tightened grimly. He had yet to prove that they were. He collected his bags and, shaking his head to a porter who offered to relieve him of them, carried them out to the car park just as his flight was being called on the Tannoy.

Ramón greeted him without surprise. He took the bags and slid them deftly into the boot of the car.

'We go back, Señor Freyton?'

'Yes,' Julian told him, 'and as fast as you know how, please.'

The chauffeur held the door for him and then walked round and slipped quickly into the driver's seat. He said, as he started the engine, 'I, too, have the feeling that all is not well, sir. I am glad that you are coming back. I will get you there as fast as it is possible and I am praying that we shall not be too late.'

Julian echoed his prayer . . . and this time didn't stop to wonder if he were being unreasonable, for his premonition of danger had become stronger, and as the powerful car roared along the flat coast road, he imagined that Margaret cried out to him in terror. Her voice seemed so close to him and her terror so real that he felt beads of perspiration break out on his brow.

'Of what,' he asked Ramón suddenly, 'are you afraid, Ramón?'

The chauffeur did not slacken speed. He answered, over his shoulder, 'Ask me rather of *whom*, Señor Freyton, and then I will tell you.'

'Well? Of whom, then?'

'Of Doña Luisa, sir,' the man told him. His strong brown hands tightened about the steering wheel. 'It is not for me to tell you such things, perhaps, but . . .' He sighed. 'I think you are the one I should tell. It concerns the Nurse Riardos, *señor*, whom I drove back to her lodgings in the city some days ago . . .' He talked on, and Julian listened with growing dismay.

It seemed to him then that he had been a blind and witless fool not to have realised the truth before. It had been plain for him to see, if he had looked in the right direction. Only he hadn't, because his long friendship with Louise and his pity for her had made him shut his eyes to any such possibility.

Ramón said quietly, 'Some years ago, Señor Freyton, Doña Luisa suffered what I think you call in English a nervous breakdown. She was very ill, and it was necessary to send her to a hospital where sick minds are treated, so that she might be cured. She was there for nearly six months, and when she returned she tried very hard to have Doña Leandra sent there, telling everyone that the old lady was more in need of such treatment than she. This was not so, *señor*. Doña Leandra broke her heart when my master died, but she is one of the real de Fonteras and she is strong. Her mind has always been clear, and it has been she who has guarded the little Don Felipe so carefully all his life.'

'I see,' Julian said. He didn't yet see the completed pattern of events, but he was beginning to see it. He wondered how much old García had known; obviously he must have been aware of Louise's mental breakdown, although he had never seen fit to mention the fact. But—he might be doing his Spanish colleague an injustice because, when he came to think about it, Dr García hadn't always been the de Fonteras' family doctor. He had been called in for the first time two years ago, to treat Felipe for some minor ailment, so it was possible that he hadn't known.

He hadn't, but Carlos had . . . Julian stiffened. Carlos had made no mention of it either. When they had gone so carefully into the question of who might have been responsible for the nearly fatal morphia injection, Carlos hadn't so much as hinted at the possibility of its being Louise. And he had lied about Nurse Riardos . . .

Leaning forward in his seat, Julian questioned Ramón, receiving the answer he had expected.

'Don Carlos ordered me not to speak of the matter to anyone, Señor Freyton,' the chauffeur told him earnestly. 'In particular, he said I was not to speak of it to you or to Dr García, in case you felt compelled to make trouble officially for Nurse Riardos, for having slept when she was on duty. She is a nice girl, and naturally I did not want her to get into trouble, so I held my tongue. I now see that it was wrong to do so.'

And how wrong, Julian thought regretfully, how terribly wrong! But he himself had been a gullible fool to have believed Carlos' story of the strangely convenient 'accident' which had befallen Nurse Riardos. That, of course, had been invented to prevent his questioning the girl; she was probably still at her lodgings, wondering fearfully whether, because she had failed in her duty, she would ever be given private nursing work again. She might not even know about the morphine injection, for Carlos would not have told her that she had been under suspicion, at one time, of having administered it.

He let his head fall into his two outstretched hands, feeling suddenly sick with disgust as he began, at last, to understand the part which Carlos had played. He had never liked or trusted the younger de Fontera, but he hadn't imagined him capable of such deception. Yet, as piece by piece the puzzle fell into place, he realised that Carlos, more than anyone else, had been responsible for what had happened.

He pretended love for the little Felipe, but he pulled the strings like a puppeteer in the background, saying one thing and doing another, and always with a smiling face, always exercising his facile charm. Felipe had been his brother's heir, he had stood between Carlos and a fortune, and so . . . Julian's mouth twisted in the darkness, as the big car, turning off the coast road, began to climb swiftly into the mountains.

Carlos, he thought, would not actively work for the evil thing he wanted, but he would see it about to happen and not lift a finger to prevent it. He had known all along about Louise, but he had kept silent, when he hadn't been lying, so that he might achieve his ends. When he hadn't been prompting and offering subtle provocation, to make sure that Louise's uneasy spirit knew no rest . . .

And Margaret was in the house, alone with the two of them, Julian reminded himself painfully. Alone, save for the little helpless Felipe and the sick and weary old lady, who had relinquished the boy's guardianship to her. He raised his head, staring into the darkness ahead of them. In his agony, the car seemed to be crawling, but, opening his mouth to urge Ramón to drive faster, he saw that the speedometer needle was hovering about the ninety-kilometre mark and he closed it again, biting off the words.

As if sensing his desperation, Ramón gestured to where, some miles in front, another car was speeding towards them, its headlights cutting a bright swathe in the surrounding blackness.

'I dare not go faster on this road, Señor Freyton,' he apologised. 'There are other cars, you see, driven recklessly like that one, and you would not want, I feel sure, that I should take too many risks.'

'No, no, of course not,' Julian assured him. The car in front of them was, as the chauffeur said, being driven with breathtaking recklessness and quite regardless of the width and condition of the steep mountain road. It came hurtling towards them, descending by a series of hairpin bends, and even at that distance, Julian could hear the screech of its protesting tyres and could picture the narrow margin of error its driver was allowing himself.

Disaster struck, even as his mind registered the fact that it must. He heard the tyres screech again and go on screeching, saw the bright beam of the headlights arch sickeningly skywards, and then, leaving the road, the other car plunged down the tree-grown slope, turning over twice and finally coming to rest on its shattered rooftop, the wheels still spinning, in the rocky fold of ground immediately below them. Strangely, although the car itself was reduced to a twisted tangle of wreckage, the headlights continued to burn, and they lit up the torn bushes and the uprooted trees which marked the path of its fall.

Ramón jammed on his brakes, skidding to a halt on the road verge. With a muffled exclamation, he jerked open the door and flung himself out of the driving seat almost in a single movement. He had a torch with him and he directed it downwards, probing the wreckage. When Julian joined him, he said, his face white and twitching, 'That is Don Carlos' car. Look, Señor Freyton, do you not recognise it?' Then, shuddering, he crossed himself. 'They cannot possibly be alive . . .'

'*They?*' Julian questioned, shaken.

Ramón looked at him, horror in his eyes. 'Doña Luisa is with him. I think it must have been she who was driving the car.' He gestured forlornly. 'See, her dress is a white blur behind the wheel. And Don Carlos drove fast, but never like that, *señor*. Never, in all the years I have known him!'

Julian hesitated for an instant. Then he started off down the slope, with Ramón following closely at his heels.

There was no sound when they reached the smashed car, and he knew, as he started to tear at the wreckage with his bare hands, that all his efforts would be futile, since it was inconceivable that anyone inside it could have survived.

He found himself wondering whether they had wanted to, but, remembering Margaret and his anxiety to get to her, he worked grimly on . . .

Doña Leandra woke to silence and an empty room. She sat up and, feeling for the switch of the lamp at her bedside, turned it on. Her tray, with the flask of coffee, cream and the two cups, stood ready and waiting for her. But Señorita Hay hadn't come, and she saw, with a feeling of faint annoyance, that unless her clock was fast, the English girl was late for her accustomed nightly visit.

Doña Leandra had come to look forward to these visits, to the shared intimacy of the coffee-drinking and the conversations they had together. She indulged in reminiscences and Margaret Hay listened to her patiently and with more interest than anyone else ever displayed. She was a charming girl, with good manners and a proper respect for age. In addition, she cared for the little Felipe with skill and devotion and had undoubtedly saved his life that night when Doña Leandra herself, in her inexperience of medical matters, hadn't realised that the boy was seriously ill.

Carlos had told her that Nurse Riardos had been responsible for the terrible error which had resulted in Felipe's collapse and . . . she sighed. He had brought her the key to the drug cupboard and had asked her to hide it, so that such a mistake could never be made again. She had hidden it with some misgivings and several times had been tempted to tell Señorita Hay that she had it, for Señorita Hay was, she felt certain, more worthy to be trusted with it than herself. Besides, she might need some of the drugs for Felipe's treatment, and if she hadn't the key which would unlock her supply, Felipe might become ill again. The only difficulty was . . . Doña Leandra shook her head irritably. Her memory had begun, of late, to fail her and she could not remember where she had put the precious key. She had looked for it in the drawer where she *thought* she had concealed it, but the key had eluded her, and now she hadn't the slightest idea where it was. She . . .

The sound of a car's engine, waking suddenly to life, distracted her for a moment. Who, she wondered, could be leaving the house at this late hour? Unless, of course, it was Carlos—the car sounded like his, and his comings and goings were often unpredictable. He had told her something about a visit he intended to pay his friends, the de Gaulas, but surely it was too late for a social call, even if the de Gaulas kept strange hours. Would he, she asked herself, marry Brigída de Gaula one of these days? She hoped he would, and her mouth compressed as she recalled, with distaste, the fact that for far too long her younger son had shown a most undesirable preference for the company of his brother's widow. Louise seemed to be indifferent to any advances he made to her, but with a woman of her type one could never be sure. Louise was not to be trusted, even with Felipe . . . Doña Leandra shivered, despite the airless warmth of the room. Least of all was she to be trusted with Felipe, although he was her son and her own flesh and blood.

There had been that occasion, last year, the old lady reminded herself, when somehow her sleeping tablets had been allowed to get into Felipe's hands. She had never been able to understand what had possessed the child to swallow them, but swallow them he had. And then there had been the time when he had almost drowned in the stream, when he was fishing, and it had been her screams which had brought help to him . . . *hers* and not his mother's, although she had been close by and must have seen him slip. Perhaps she was wicked and uncharitable to imagine what she did about Louise, because she loved the boy, there could be no doubt of that, and there had never been any proof, but . . .

A clock struck, on the landing outside. A trifle resentfully, Doña Leandra counted the strokes, glancing at her own small travelling clock, to make certain that it hadn't gained. It was, she saw, exactly right. And yet Señorita Hay hadn't come. Like all the British, she was very punctual, and besides, it was part of her duty to pay these nightly calls on her, to make certain that she was all right. She did her duty most conscientiously as a rule, so there must be some reason for her lateness.

Doña Leandra sat bolt upright in the great four-poster bed, her old heart beating very fast. There could be only one reason for Señorita Hay's lateness, and the reason must be Felipe. Perhaps he was ill again, perhaps something had happened to cause him to suffer a relapse . . . she considered ringing for María, but dismissed the idea almost at once. María was quite useless in a crisis: if anything was wrong, she would be better to go and see for herself. She reached for her dressing gown, struggled into it and climbed out of the high bed. As an afterthought, she rang the bell that would summon María and set off shakily down the long, dimly-lit corridor which led to Felipe's sickroom.

She smelled the gas the instant she opened the door, and acted with courage and promptitude. She had the windows open and the gas fire turned off by the time her cries for help had roused the household and brought the servants to her side.

Then she collapsed, but not before she had seen, to her heartfelt relief, that Felipe was still breathing . . .

Margaret returned very slowly and almost reluctantly to awareness of her surroundings. Blurred shapes flitted about her, seeming oddly unreal, and someone was evidently attempting to give her artificial respiration in a rather painful and unskilled manner, for she could feel hands pressing hard on her back, being released and pressing again, harder and more awkwardly than before. But she felt too ill to beg whoever it was to stop, too spent and exhausted to breathe for herself, and although she heard voices quite near her, she couldn't make out what they were saying. And she couldn't remember anything very clearly, except that she had had another nightmare and Louise de Fontera had, for some inexplicable reason, been part of it.

It wasn't until she heard Julian's voice calling her name that she made any serious effort to rouse herself. There was such agony in his voice, such tenderness, that she had to respond to it, had to make the effort to open her eyes in order to see if he was really there. When she saw him, she felt a great happiness fill her, a great peace. She wanted to sleep again, but he would not let her.

'Speak to me, Margaret,' he bade her, over and over again, so insistently that she obeyed him.

'I love you, Julian,' she whispered, and then, not knowing why she had said it or from whence the memory had come, she said in a husky, unrecognisable whisper, 'I rang the bell . . . I *did* manage to . . . ring it, this time. But no one came. No one . . .'

To her surprise, it was Sister Teresa who answered her, although evidently, since it was Julian she spoke to, he must have repeated her words. 'The lead to the bell in Felipe's room was cut, Doctor. That was why I did not hear it.'

Margaret saw that they were looking at each other, with a knowledge in their eyes which she did not share, and then Julian told her she must sit up, and Sister Teresa, her smile pitying and tremulous, was holding a glass to her lips.

'Drink this, child,' she urged. 'It will make you feel a little better.'

She drank submissively, but didn't really feel better until Julian lifted her in his arms and held her to him.

'Don't worry, my darling,' he told her gently. 'You're quite safe. I'm with you and I'm not going to leave you again. But you've got to *try* to wake up. Please, my little love, try!'

'I'm trying, Julian,' she assured him, and then, suddenly afraid, 'What about Felipe? Julian, is he all right?'

'He's better than you are,' Julian told her gruffly.

'But . . .' Memory was returning now, but everything

was confused. 'What *happened*? Why was I asleep?'

'You shall hear the whole story,' he promised, 'as soon as you wake up.'

But it was, in fact, another twenty-four hours before she was fit to hear it. Julian told her in a flat, unhappy voice, sitting at her bedside, and Margaret listened incredulously, still scarcely able to take it in.

'I think,' she said, when he had done, 'that I would rather forget it, Julian. If one can ever forget such a story.'

He smiled then and gathered her to him. 'As soon as you're well enough to travel, I'm taking you back to London, darling. It will be easier to forget it there, for both of us.'

As always, he was right. In time, the bitter memories faded and only the happy ones remained. But it was not until a year after their marriage that Margaret and Julian returned to Spain.

The luxurious black limousine met them at the airport, with a beaming Ramón at the wheel. Seated in regal dignity in the back of the splendid car, old Doña Leandra bowed to them graciously. A strange young man, whom she afterwards came to know as Don Jaime de Fontera, kissed Margaret's hand and welcomed her politely, turning to shake Julian's, his manner grave and respectful.

And then, from the reception hall, a small figure emerged, looking about him with furrowed brows. Seeing them, Felipe ran over to them and hurled himself ecstatically into Margaret's waiting arms.

He ran fleetly and without any sign of a limp, the small, dark head held proudly erect. If he was still a trifle over-thin, that was all; his face was healthily tanned, his arms strong.

'Oh, Sister Margarita, I thought you hadn't come! I was there, waiting for you, and I was so much afraid you hadn't come . . .'

Margaret clasped him to her. 'Did you want me to come, Felipe?' she asked, her throat tight.

'Of course I did,' the boy told her eagerly. 'I want to take you—both you and Mr Freyton—to Castello Delmonte, so that you may see how well I can swim now.' He looked from Margaret's face to Julian's. 'You'll come, won't you?' he pleaded.

Julian grinned. Tucking Margaret's hand into the crook of his arm, he led her to the car. 'We'll come,' he answered. 'Castello Delmonte is a very special place for us, Felipe. We'll be very glad to go there again, with you, won't we, darling?'

Margaret echoed his smile. 'Yes,' she said, 'we will.'

They got into the car and Doña Leandra held out both hands in welcome. 'Señora Freyton,' she said, 'I am pleased to see you again. But to us, I think, you will always be Sister Margarita. I hope you do not mind?'

Margaret glanced at her husband. 'No,' she answered gaily, 'of course I don't mind, Doña Leandra. I'm *glad*.'

Felipe plumped himself down beside her. 'She's *my* Sister Margarita,' he stated firmly, and reached for her hand.

Doctor Nurse Romances

Romance in the wide world of medicine

Amongst the intense emotional pressures of modern medical life, doctors and nurses often find romance. Read about their lives and loves in the other two Doctor Nurse titles available this month.

A CANDLE IN THE DARK
Grace Read

Young Sister Bryony Clemence and the new surgical registrar Grant Stirling rub each other up the wrong way whenever they meet, but is it only chance that dictates that they should meet so often?

DECISION FOR A NURSE
Jean Evans

When Sister Clare Summers accompanies a badly injured patient to his home in France she believes herself to be in love. Why should the arrogant Dr Alain Duval be so determined to make her doubt this belief?

Mills & Boon
the rose of romance

Doctor Nurse Romances

Romance in modern medical life

Read more about the lives and loves of doctors and nurses in the fascinatingly different backgrounds of contemporary medicine. These are the three Doctor Nurse romances to look out for next month.

HOSPITAL ACROSS THE BRIDGE
Lisa Cooper

BACHELOR DOCTOR
Sonia Deane

NEW SURGEON AT ST LUCIAN'S
Elizabeth Houghton

Buy them from your usual paperback stockist, or write to: Mills & Boon Reader Service, P.O. Box 236, Thornton Rd, Croydon, Surrey CR9 3RU, England. Readers in South Africa-write to: Mills & Boon Reader Service of Southern Africa, Private Bag X3010, Randburg, 2125.

Mills & Boon
the rose of romance

How to join in a whole new world of romance

It's very easy to subscribe to the Mills & Boon Reader Service. As a regular reader, you can enjoy a whole range of special benefits. Bargain offers. Big cash savings. Your own free Reader Service newsletter, packed with knitting patterns, recipes, competitions, and exclusive book offers.

We send you the very latest titles each month, postage and packing free – no hidden extra charges. There's absolutely no commitment – you receive books for only as long as you want.

We'll send you details. Simply send the coupon – or drop us a line for details about the Mills & Boon Reader Service Subscription Scheme.
Post to: Mills & Boon Reader Service, P.O. Box 236, Thornton Road, Croydon, Surrey CR9 3RU, England.
*Please note: READERS IN SOUTH AFRICA please write to: Mills & Boon Reader Service of Southern Africa, Private Bag X3010, Randburg 2125, S. Africa.

Please send me details of the Mills & Boon Subscription Scheme.

NAME (Mrs/Miss) _____ EP3

ADDRESS _____

_____

COUNTY/COUNTRY _____ POST/ZIP CODE _____

BLOCK LETTERS, PLEASE

Mills & Boon
the rose of romance